The Switch-Up

ISABELLA SHAUNTE

Palmetto Publishing Group, LLC
Charleston, SC

Copyright © 2017 by Isabella Shaunte

All rights reserved. No portion of this book may be reproduced, stored in a retrieval system, or transmitted in any form by any means–electronic, mechanical, photocopy, recording, or other–except for brief quotations in printed reviews, without prior permission of the publisher.

For more information regarding special discounts for bulk purchases, please contact Palmetto Publishing Group at Info@PalmettoPublishingGroup.com.

ISBN-13: 978-1-944313-42-5
ISBN-10: 1-944313-42-7

Dedication

*This book goes out to Tevin Smith.
Thank you for inspiring me to write this story.*

I SPLASHED WATER ON MY FACE and then looked at myself in the mirror, trying to figure out how I was going to get through the night knowing she was in my house alone, in my bed, on the other side of that door. The urge to climb into bed with her was killing me, reaching all the way down to my Joe boxers. I looked at the door when I heard her snoring and gave a little laugh. The girl had no shame in expressing herself. If I told her she snored like a congested walrus, she'd probably laugh it off and be like, "Boy, shut up, it's a natural thing and I can't help it." She never took what I said to her personally; that's why I liked her so much.

I looked back to the mirror and my smile vanished. The feeling I was beginning to have for her was so wrong but felt so right—well, on my end it felt right. I wasn't sure about her thoughts on the matter, and I couldn't help but wonder: If I climbed in that bed, would she let me hold her in my arms until the sun came up? If I kissed her, would she kiss me back? I didn't even want to have sex with her, even though I knew her body would feel satisfied afterward. I guess you could call it a guilty pleasure.

I didn't know if he wanted to get back with her or not. It had never been my intention to come between their relationship, but it had all happened so quickly and unexpectedly that I honestly hadn't seen it coming. I don't know if we'll be together, go our separate ways, or pretend it never happened. Will I regret possibly ruining a good friendship by trying to cross the line?

Just A Homey

It was a normal day at work in the warehouse for us: packing, labeling, and shipping boxes.

My coworker of a year and a half, Adrianna Castillo, a.k.a. Adrian, was returning from a trip home to Puerto Rico. She was always traveling somewhere; whenever she felt like it, she just packed her bags and went, with no hesitation. That was the privileges a single person without kids had. I didn't have any kids either, but I did have a girl waiting at home for me, and I couldn't travel anywhere without Crystal.

Without looking at the doorway, I knew Adrian was near because a few other employees cheered her name in unison like Norm from the TV show *Cheers*. "There she goes; my day just gotten times better!" I heard one of the guys say.

I glanced over and watched her give high fives and

hugs as she walked toward the doorway. A crowd began to form around her, and another employee asked her how the trip was and what she did. I continued to load my truck, knowing I would get my chance to talk to Adrian later. She had the crowd going for about fifteen minutes before saying she would tell everyone more later.

I admired the respect she received in the workplace from all the men and women. She wasn't too hard to get along with, she was always easygoing and outspoken. She also had a temper like a volcano: smooth and calm in the beginning, and then she'd begin to rumble, and then she'd explode. I'd only seen it once, about a year ago, when an old coworker had started stalking her because she wouldn't give him a chance to be with her. It was all fun and games until the dude followed her home from work. She called me when she saw his car parked a few blocks from her house. She owned a gun but was too afraid to use it. I called the cops for her and met them at her house to help prove that the guy was out of control. I even went to court with her to get a restraining order.

I was locking up my truck when I felt her pat my shoulder and say, "Omar, what's up, homey?"

I gave her a dap. "What's up? How you doing? How was your vacation?"

"It was great. Anything that has me away from here is great." She looked around and asked, "Where the boss man at?"

"He left early."

"Good," she said as she pulled the ends of her Coca-Cola polo out of her pants and fixed her jet-black hair in a bun before putting her hat back on.

Adrian was White, Puerto Rican, and Black. All her ethnicities showed in her features. She had the tan White-girl complexion; the Puerto Rican accent; and the Black-girl attitude, hips, and curves. For an African-American brother, that combination was heaven-sent. She was neither skinny nor fat; she stood at an average five foot seven and was thirty years old. Adrian had beautiful skin, perfect lips, and a beautiful smile. I couldn't understand why she chose to be single.

"You working with me today?"

I pulled the truck keys out my pocket and said, "Yeah. Mr. Pumer wasn't sure if you were going to come back, since you told him you'd be quitting soon. So, he asked me to take over."

She smiled. "Unfortunately, that time hasn't come yet."

We both got into the truck. I started the engine and began asking more about her trip. "So, what'd you do during your visit home?"

"I hung out with my family. Everyone's doing good, by the way." She buckled her seatbelt. "And I hooked up with some old friends."

"Old friends or old flames?" I teased.

She shook her head. "Just friends. Not old flames I

could have, but I didn't."

I pulled out of the parking lot and onto the road, then said, "I've told you to stop that fornicating and going back in the past."

Adrian rolled her eyes "Whatever. I can do what I want—I'm single, and even if I did have sex or do anything with an ex, that's what us single people do until we find something new to do."

I glanced at her and said, "That sounds so sad coming from you. You act like you have to be single, you could get a man if you really wanted one."

"You right I can 'get' a man. Any female can 'get' a man. Finding one that's loyal, honest, respectable, hardworking, without kids, and not a weed head, is hard to do nowadays."

"Hey, that's not true! I'm everything you just said, and I'm sure I'm not the only one in this world with those qualities."

She glance at me and said, "You're right. But just like you, all the others are already taken. The married ones want to act single. The ones that are supposed to be taken, one of them is acting single. Everyone should just be happy with staying single. Less drama, less stress."

I hated that Adrian's mind was set because of a few bad dates and relationships from her younger days. "Mike was willing to run to the end of the world and back for you," I teased, referring to her stalker.

She rolled her eyes and said, "Michael was controlling, a psycho, and he just couldn't handle rejection."

"I really didn't think he was that bad. He just knew what he wanted and tried his best to get it, meaning he would've been loyal and hardworking, and he would have given you anything you asked for. What was the problem with that?"

She frowned. "Are you saying I should have dated Michael because he was stalking me? Are you serious, Omar? That dude only knew me for a week, and within that time he found out where I lived, my phone number, and where I went. That's not normal attraction—that's fatal attraction, and that was very scary. Never will I date a guy who will go that far for my attention. Geesh! Being in a relationship isn't that serious."

She had a point. I remembered a time when Michael told anyone in the warehouse who would listen that he would kill and die for Adrian. And it had only been his second day at the job.

I parked the truck at our first drop-off destination and said, "Adrian, all I'm saying is I want to see you happy with someone. You always doing things by yourself and for yourself. It would be nice to hear you doing it with your man or future husband."

Adrian hopped out of the truck and replied, "Who said I'm not happy? I'm fine being all by myself."

"I know you want somebody to call on when you're bored or need someone to talk to."

She smiled at me and said, "That what I got you for, homey."

I opened the back of the truck, let the ramp down, and said, "Besides me. There are a lot of things you can't do with me because I'm taken. I can't take you out and wine and dine you, I can't buy you gifts for no particular reason at all, and we can't have sex morning, noon, and night."

Adrian laughed, "We could if we were those types of people. And I know you and Crystal aren't having sex morning, noon, and night. You work in the mornings, she works at noon. Now that I think about I guess you're right about the night part."

Unfortunately, she was wrong about the night part. Crystal had been complaining so much about how tired she was that it was tough for me to at least get a quickie in before I went to work. Even on her off days, lately.

I pulled two hand trucks down and said, "That's not my point. My point is, I want to see you with somebody before the year of the rats comes."

Adrian giggled and hit me in my arm. "Shut up."

We walked into the convenience store, restocked it, then continued our conversation once we got back inside the truck.

"I am going to set you up with somebody, Adrian."

"I don't want to be hooked up, Omar. I can find someone to be with on my own."

"Come on, I know someone who'll be just what

you're looking for."

"Who's that?"

I glanced at her and said, "My little brother, Kennedy. I mean, he not little—we're eight months apart, he was premature. He's twenty-nine, an accountant, looks like me, no kids, no drama."

Adrian studied me for a minute. "Didn't you tell me he peed the bed until he was thirteen and got bullied all the time in grade school?"

I laughed at the memories her questions brought to my mind and said, "Yeah, but he's changed. He took a few martial art classes and got a little backbone. He can be a little bigheaded, but I think you can handle him."

Adrian growled, "Just because I can handle him doesn't mean I want to deal with him."

"Come on, Adrian," I pleaded. "He's a good guy. Come to my house next week for dinner; He's in town on a vacation from work I'll invite him and you two can see if there's a connection."

She gave a heavy sigh and said, "Okay, I'll give him a shot."

The Hookup

"Crystal! Is everything ready yet?" I yelled from my bedroom closet.

"It will be in a minute—the peach cobbler's almost done," she called back.

"Great!"

I pulled a fresh pair of jeans and t-shirt out of the closet and placed them on the bed. I was too excited about this hookup. I was acting as if I were the one being hooked up with Adrian, like I had to dress to impress for some reason. I rubbed my face with my hands and wondered if I needed to shave. Looking in the dresser mirror, I scrutinized the left side of my face and then the right.

"Baby, what are you doing?" Crystal asked from behind me.

I studied Crystal's refection in the mirror; she had on jean shorts and a tank top. "That's not what you're wearing to dinner, is it?"

She looked down at her clothes. "What's wrong with what I'm wearing?"

I turned around and said, "Can you put on something more decent, like a sundress or something? We're having guests for dinner."

Crystal frowned. "It's just your brother and your coworker. It's not like they First Lady Michelle Obama and President Barack Obama."

I growled, "Just do it, Crystal, please."

She threw her hands up in the air, flipped her fake hair, and said, "Fine, Omar, I'll change clothes."

I watched her stomp out the door.

I met Crystal at a train station when she'd been in the transitioning stage of moving to the city. She'd been lost, so she asked me for directions. Some other person had given her the wrong directions. I was going her way, so I rode the train with her until she got to her destination. I couldn't say we'd connected right then and there; from the short conversation, we shared on the train, I could tell she was spoiled, and when she told me she was part of Alpha Kappa Alpha, my hunch was confirmed. All she did was talk about how she was going to Georgia Tech and how much money she was going to be making when she finished school. Nothing she said made me want to take things further with her, but because she had a petite body and a nice smile, I'd given her my number when she'd asked for it.

Crystal Simmons was twenty-nine and had moved

The Switch-Up

to Atlanta from Ohio. After graduating from Georgia Tech with a biochemistry major, she'd gotten a job at Piedmont Hospital. She'd been working hard to get with the CDC. I didn't understand why, especially since she made good money where she was. I guess like the rapper T.I.P says, "If it ain't about the money."

She'd called me a few days later, chitchatting about her day. I never asked her out because I wasn't really interested in her in that way. Kevin Hart had been in town, and Crystal asked me to go with her. I wanted to see his show but hadn't had the time, they were front row seats and I didn't have to pay for them. So, I told her yeah.

We'd gone out to eat, and she had talked more about herself and how happy she was to be out with someone "different." I asked her what she meant by different; she told me she usually didn't date guys with "average" jobs. That she was used to guys who had careers and owned their own houses. Now some people would have taken offense to what she'd said, but personally I didn't care what she thought about me working at the Coca-Cola factory. It hadn't stopped me from getting a condo in Buckhead, owning a car, or doing what I wanted to do when I wanted to do it.

I hadn't approached the night like it was a date; my plan had been to take her home and block her number so she would leave me the hell alone. Somehow, one goodbye handshake led to a relationship that had now lasted a little over two years. I don't know how it happened—maybe it was the sex or the alcohol, or just plain boredom.

We didn't have any kids or live together, even though she stayed over almost every night and I had more of her things in my closet and bathroom than my own. I never asked her to move in with me, and I didn't plan on doing it either. Don't get me wrong, I did care for her, but she had a bad habit of getting on my nerves by nagging and complaining when she couldn't get her way. I didn't think I could live with that the rest of my life, if we were to get married or have kids, I would've had to. Thankfully, she hadn't pressured me on those two things yet. She said she wanted to get married but didn't want kids. According to Crystal, having kids would ruin her body and mess up her career goals. Since it that was not in my plan, so it wasn't a big deal when she told me that.

Things between us weren't bad; she did know how to cook, and we did have a few things in common besides sex and alcohol—we both liked trying different food, TV shows, movies, and big events. When she wasn't getting on my nerves, Crystal was fun to be around. We went to parties and sports events; she was always the center of attention. Whenever a big event was happening in town, she had to be there.

Kennedy thought our relationship was a disaster waiting to happen.

Now my little brother on the other hand, had tried

so hard to be a part of the "in crowd" when we were in elementary school. He would have sold his soul for people to pay more attention to him. He did whatever they wanted, whenever they said so, not knowing he was just a puppet and they were his masters. I'd tried to tell him that his so-called friends were using him to help them pass classes or do their dirty work. But he wouldn't listen to me because sometimes I was one of them. I used to bully him constantly when he told me no. I used to lock him in the closet because I knew he was scared of the dark. He would run around the house crying, asking my mom and dad to make me stop. My mom would cradle him like a baby and tell me to stop tormenting him, and my dad would tell him to man up.

Still looking in the mirror, I laughed out loud just thinking about it.

But I had to admit that Kennedy had gotten the last laugh. When we reached high school, he got rid of his so-called friends and focused on his work. He graduated as valedictorian, with a 4.0 GPA. I was so proud of him. He had gone to college and had become a certified public accountant; he was making some big money and working with some well-known people. And the fact that he was wife- and childless had him rolling around town like he was part of Cash Money Records. He had the big house and fancy car and first-class trips. He used to send our parents on cruises and give them plane tickets to places all around the world; since they were both retired and we were both grown, they could enjoy their lives. I never asked Kennedy for anything, but he did help me get the condo. He had offered to buy our parents a new house, they thought it was unnecessary so they declined his offer, so he remodeled their house instead, updated their appliances, and installed a fireplace.

They hadn't used that fireplace until one Sunday dinner, six years ago. Kennedy had lecturing them about not using it, so Dad fired it up to shut him up. Sometime that night, Kennedy had come into my room complaining about his asthma acting up. He was twenty-three at the time, so I knew he wasn't simply overreacting; this was something serious. I'd stepped out of bed, and my head had begun to throb. Kennedy began to hyperventilate. I told him to open the window, but he was too weak and I was also getting light-headed. I picked up a lamp from the nightstand and threw it against the window, shattering the glass. I ordered Kennedy to climb out; with every breath he took, he asked me to get our parents. As I called for our parents, ran to the hallway, and immediately began to gag. Causing me to ran back into the room, climbed out the window, and puked on the grass.

Kennedy was next to me, still trying to suck in as much oxygen as he could while demanding that I get Mom and Dad out of the house. The neighbors began to come out of their homes. I kept trying to tell Kennedy that we couldn't go back inside—the carbon monoxide was too strong and we needed to get help. But he wasn't hearing it. He staggered to the back house, falling and coughing with every step he took. I yelled at the neighbor for help before chasing after my brother. When I reached Kennedy, he was climbing into our parents' bedroom window. As soon as his foot hit the floor, he passed out. I pulled the blinds down with the help of a few neighbors, helped me dragged all one hundred and forty-five pounds of him back outside.

The first responders came and resuscitated Kennedy; unfortunate our parents didn't make it. It broke my heart but damn near killed Kennedy and almost tore us apart. He had started blaming me for not trying hard enough to save them; then he'd started blaming himself for making them light the fireplace. It had taken three years of counseling for us to get our brotherly bond back. With our parents gone, we were all we had to get by.

I loved my brother. We chatted on the phone when he wasn't busy; it had been two and a half years since I'd seen him, he'd been doing most of his business Los. Angeles. That was one of the reasons I was so excited about this get-together.

I walked into my bathroom and took a hot shower. After, feeling fresh, I stood in front of the sink and examined my face again; I looked pretty young for twenty-nine going on thirty. I had a face like the actor Larenz Tate—it never seemed to age. I guessed it was true when they said black don't crack. Kennedy was younger but looked older and more like our father, while I resembled our mother.

I walked in the bathroom pushed Crystal's makeup and hair products to the side and decided to shave and put on some fresh cologne.

After dressing, I walked into the kitchen and saw Crystal pulling the cobbler out of the oven. She had changed into a casual sleeveless summer dress. I kissed her cheek and thanked her.

She snarled, "I still don't see why I had to change."

I exhaled loudly. "Don't argue with me right now, okay?"

The doorbell rang, and I told Crystal to start setting the kitchen table while I answered the door.

"What's up, homey?"

I looked down at Adrian and asked, "This what you call dressed to impress?"

She glanced down at her blue jeans and Aée'ropostale t-shirt and said, "I wore heels, there's nothing wrong with what I'm wearing."

"Why didn't you wear a dress?"

Adrian smacked her lips and replied, "It's not like we're at a restaurant."

I stared at her ponytail. "At least let your hair down."

Adrian frowned, then shook her head no. "There is nothing wrong with me, Omar. Now let me in this place before I go back home."

I stepped aside to let her in, then closed the door. I playfully tugged on her ponytail and whined, "Take it down, please."

She pushed my hand away and hit me in the shoulder. "Stop it! You messing up my hair."

"It's impossible to mess up a ponytail. It's the laziest hairstyle a woman can do."

Adrian redid her ponytail, giggled, and said, "Shut up, Omar. I'm comfortable. If your brother doesn't like me now, then he won't like me later."

Crystal walked into the living room, stood by my side, smiled, and said, "Hello, you must be Andria."

Adrian gave a little smile. "No, Crystal, it's Adrian, short for Adrianna."

Crystal and Adrian had never actually met each other, and I never talked much to Crystal about Adrian because I knew Crystal would swear we were too close and that something was going on between us. When I hung out with Adrian, it was always during work hours or when Crystal was at work. I didn't know why I felt I had to do that—Crystal had plenty of male friends that she hung out with from time to time. I didn't mind. I'd met the guys she hung with, and I didn't feel threatened by any of them.

Adrian knew about Crystal because I constantly talked about her at work—the good, the bad, and the ugly. Plus, when I needed a woman's point of view on something, Adrian seemed to know it all.

Crystal shook Adrian's hand and said, "Sorry, it's nice to meet you, Adrianna."

"Same here, Crystal. Love your dress."

"Thank you. Nice heels."

"Thank you."

I clapped my hands and said, "Enough of the girl talk. Kennedy should be here soon. Crystal, is everything ready for dinner?"

She growled, "For the thousandth time, yes, baby."

I had no clue what her problem was; I assumed it was that time of the month because she was really funkin' up my mood and killing' my vibe. Trying not to embarrass her in front of Adrian, I asked, "Do we need to talk about something?"

She frowned. "No, why?"

"I'm just trying to find out where this attitude's coming from and how we can fix it."

Adrian excused herself to the restroom.

Crystal snapped, "Do not embarrass me in front of guests, Omar."

I arched my eyebrow at her. "How am I embarrassing you? I just asked you a simple question and you caught an attitude."

"Yes, a simple question that I've answered five times in the last hour. What are you so excited about anyway?"

I forgot I hadn't told Crystal my plans to hook up Adrian and Kennedy. I hadn't even told my brother because I knew he'd probably back out of it. I told Crystal about my plan and asked her not to mention it or ruin it for me.

She smiled. "Okay, I won't spoil it." Then she gave me a peck on the lips. "I'll go set the table."

I smiled back, then tapped her on the butt as she walked away. "Good girl."

I was looking out the window when Adrian came up behind me and said, "You acting like a kid on Christmas Eve who just can't wait to open his present."

I turned to her. "I can't wait until you meet Kennedy; this is going to be a match made in heaven."

Adrian smirked. "Whatever you say, Mr. Million-Dollar Matchmaker. I'm going to help your girlfriend set the table."

I gazed back out the window and said, "Thank you."

My eyes lit up as soon as I saw Kennedy's red BMW 3 Series coupe drive into the parking lot. I ran out the door and tackled him right as he stepped out of his car. I lifted him a few feet off the grown. He had gained so much weight since he'd started working out—he had to be at least two-sixty now. But that didn't stop me from giving him a bear hug.

Kennedy gave a little grin and said, "Aww, come on, O, ease up on the bear hug! You're killing me."

I laughed and patted him on the back. "What's up, baby brother? I missed you."

Kennedy straightened his Gucci polo shirt and said, "I missed you too, Omar." He closed his car door.

I placed my arm over his shoulders and asked, "What's new? I see from the car that everything's going well with the job."

"Everything's good."

Kennedy pressed his shirt and pleated pants again and I said, "What, are you a pretty boy now, afraid to get a little wrinkle in your shirt?"

He chuckled. "You just messing up my gear." He studied me and said, "I see you still don't know how to dress your age."

I looked over my streetwear. "Hey, I'm still young! Just because I don't wear four-hundred-dollar shirts don't mean I don't know how to dress fresh."

Kennedy corrected me, "It was six. And this is how grown men dress."

"No, that's how Carlton Banks from *The Fresh Prince of Bel-Air* dresses. You need to let me take you shopping one day, and then maybe you'll finally get a girl."

Kennedy rolled his eyes. "Whatever, O, I'm doing fine without one."

I crossed my arm across my chest. "Oh really. I don't understand why you won't date. You been working hard since you got your degree—don't you think it's time to find someone to share your success with?"

He looked at me and said, "I do date; I'm just not looking to be tied down right now. And don't you start looking for me, Omar."

I smiled and placed my arm back around his

shoulders as we walked toward the condo. "All right, I'll let the women come to you."

I opened the door and announced, "O and K Kingston in the house!"

Crystal and Adrian came from the kitchen, and I introduced Kennedy to Adrian.

Kennedy shook Adrian's hand. "Nice to meet you." Then he shook Crystal's hand. "It's nice to see you again."

I clapped my hands together and said, "All right, everybody, let's eat." We all sat down and ate the veggie lasagna Crystal had cooked.

I decided to get the show on the road before Kennedy tried to leave. "So, Kennedy, tell me how everything's going in the accountant world."

After wiping his face with his napkin, he answered, "Everything's going well, Omar. Are you still working at that factory?"

"Yeah, I'm still there—twelve years strong."

Kennedy gave a little smirk. "When are you going to do something better and make some real money? You have a degree in business—why not use it?"

He was right—I did have a business degree. Unlike him, I went to a community college and got my degree to please my parents. I'd been working at the factory since the twelfth grade. I wasn't making millions, but I thought I was making a decent amount for the time I'd been there.

Kennedy sighed. "I don't think you should settle for

this job and get too comfortable. There's always something better out there."

Crystal agreed with him, saying, "I try to tell him that all the time, to find a job that pays more money so he can better himself and be happy."

I narrowed my eyes and started to defend myself because these two attacking me had not been part of the plan.

Adrian stood up for me instead. "Who said he's not happy? Omar has worked in every department in that factory, and he does a great job doing it. He has gotten numerous awards and plenty of recognition on the job. I do agree that he can do better—and I believe he will at the factory. I can see him working in corporate even as the CEO. Just because he's not making a million-dollar salary doesn't mean he's settling. He's doing what he loves, his bills are getting paid, he has a roof over his head and food in his stomach, his bank account's not empty, and that's all that should matter. Whether these two say it or not, Omar, I'm proud of you for doing your job for the love of it and not for money."

I couldn't help but smile a big Kool-Aid grin at her encouragement and the faith she had in me I was so flabbergasted. I leaned across the table, gave her a dap, and said, "Thanks, homey. I appreciate that."

She wasn't too enthusiastic when she replied, "No problem." I could tell she was getting irritated by Kennedy and Crystal attacking me. Those two attacking me about my lifestyle was nothing new; I'd seen and heard about the problems most financially successful people like them went through on a yearly basis. I didn't know how Kennedy had gotten to be so money-hungry because our parents hadn't raised us that way. We hadn't been poor, but we for damn sure weren't rich. Even though we'd stayed in a middle-class neighborhood, our parents had always told us to work for what we wanted and to be happy doing it.

Like the Notorious B.I.G. said: more money, more problems. I didn't have any problems, and I was truly happy about it.

Kennedy looked at me and said, "I am proud of my brother."

Crystal agreed, "I'm proud of my baby; I just can't wait until he moves up in the company so we can be living life like the Jefferson's." She laughed.

Adrian smirked and said, "Oh, what a joy that will bring for you two."

I chuckled at her sarcasm; I had to get the conversation off me, but Kennedy beat me to it. He looked at Adrian and asked, "So you work for the factory too?"

She rolled her eyes and said, "As a matter of fact, I do. Is that a problem?"

Kennedy shook his head. "It's your life—you can do as you please. How long have you been working there?"

"Almost two years."

"How long are you planning on being there? Are

you waiting to move up too?"

Adrian narrowed her eyes at him, and the black-girl side of her came out. "I surely am; I'll be working at the factory until the day I die."

I burst into laughter at both her comment and the expression on my brother's face. I had to correct her before he believed the words coming out of her mouth. "That's not true, Kennedy. She just working at the factory until she graduates to become a dentist—an orthodontist, to be exact."

"How much longer will that take?" Kennedy asked her.

Still being sarcastic, she said, "Five years."

I corrected her, "Four months."

"Oh, okay. I mean, you have to start somewhere, I guess."

Adrian looked at him with confusion. "So, you telling me the only job you ever had was this accountant one?"

Kennedy shook his head. "No, but I always had a job that only dealt with the requirement of me handling money. I worked at banks and as a cash room clerk. That way, when I finished school and got a job in my field, I'd have the skills and basic knowledge necessary for the position before I even started it."

Without being sarcastic Adrian said, "That's interesting."

Impressed also, Crystal smiled and said, "Very interesting and smart. I wish someone would've told me to do that when I was younger." I couldn't help but roll my eyes.

Kennedy looked at me. "I've been trying to tell Omar about it for years, but he won't listen to me."

"I told him maybe he should go back to school," she commented.

Getting irritated, I looked at her and said, "I told you I don't want to go back to school, Crystal. And Kennedy, I've told you I don't need your help. I'm satisfied with the way my life's going right now. It would be nice if you two would stop jumping on me about it."

They both apologized, then Kennedy asked Adrian what she was mixed with.

I answered for her, "White, black, and Puerto Rican."

Kennedy asked if she could speak Spanish.

She glanced over at him and answered, "Believe it or not, it's my second language."

Kennedy frowned. "I don't understand, how can you be from there and not speak the language?"

Adrian snapped, "I was born in Puerto Rico but was raised here in Atlanta. My father is Latino, and my mother is black and white. Maybe that will help you understand it better." Not wanting to talk anymore, she stood up and said, "Dinner was good, but it's time for me to go."

I stood up too and walked with Adrian to her car.

"Do *not* try to hook me up with your arrogant brother."

I gave a little laugh. "I know he's a little arrogant. But he really is a good guy—he just doesn't know how to shut up sometimes."

Opening her car door, she said, "I don't like the way your girlfriend and he kept ganging up on you because you don't live the life they want you to. Even though they were talking to *you*, I felt offended as well." She growled, "I hate people like them. Looking down on other people just because they make a few dollars more—and then they end up in debt because they don't know how to handle it."

I patted her on the shoulder. "Calm down, Adrian. Kennedy and Crystal didn't mean any harm, and they both apologized."

"I don't care. I still don't like it."

I held out my arm to give her a hug; she stepped in. I held her close and said, "All right, I won't try to hook you up with Kennedy. Thank you for having my back in there."

She smiled at me as we pulled apart and said, "Always."

***

"What is her problem? Would you date her?"

Kennedy looked at Crystal confused then asked, "Are you talking about Adrianna?"

"Yeah, would you date a woman like her?"

"She's attractive, but dating her? I'm not too sure about that."

Crystal snickered. "You don't look like the type who would date a wannabe."

Kennedy smirked. "I wouldn't call her a 'wannabe.' She'll be graduating soon." He paused. "Why'd you ask if I would date her?"

"Omar was trying to hook you up with her; he thinks you two would be a perfect match. But I know you the type of guy who wants his woman to have her priorities together, working at a real job, making real money." Crystal smiled at him. "Like me, for example."

Kennedy chuckled. "I must admit, I do prefer the women I date to already have an established career." He took a drink of water. "And I'm not really planning on being hooked up with anyone right now."

"What are you waiting for? You got a career making big money, the cars and the big house—and not to mention, the look, too. Trust me, there are plenty of women in this world who fit what you're looking for. You just have to keep your eyes wide open."

He raised an eyebrow and said, "I'll keep that in mind, when I find her."

Crystal smiled before sipping her drink and saying, "Smart move."

When I stepped into the kitchen, Kennedy got up from his chair and said, "I think I should be going, too."

Crystal began to clean off the table as if nothing out

of the ordinary had occurred. I walked Kennedy out the door, and he asked me to walk him to his car.

"What's up?"

"I want to apologize if I insulted you in any way in there. You know I don't mean no harm—I just want the best for you."

I gave him a hug. "I know, man. Like I said, I'm doing good. Just don't mention it anymore, all right?"

Kennedy smiled. "All right. What is up with this hooking up plan you have? Crystal told me you were trying to hook me up with your Adrianna."

I laughed and said, "I told her not to tell you! But it doesn't matter now; she doesn't want you."

Kennedy frowned. "Why not?"

"She say you not her type."

"Not her type? What she want—a thug or a bum?"

I teased him, "No, she just doesn't want you. She says you're too arrogant."

Not liking my response, Kennedy pulled his cell phone out of his pocket and said, "I am *not* arrogant. What's her number?"

I knew I shouldn't have told him that Adrian wasn't interested because I knew he would try to prove her wrong. Since he'd been a doormat when we were little, he still felt as if he had to prove any and every one that he was good enough to do any and everything they could do—and better.

Adrian had made it clear that she didn't want to

have anything to do with my brother, and I'd promised her I wouldn't keep trying to hook them up. I shook my head and said, "Sorry, bro, I can't do it. She asked me to stay out of it."

Kennedy sighed. "Well give her mine; I want to talk to her."

I had a feeling he didn't really want to be with Adrian. He told me earlier he didn't want to be hooked up — he just wanted to prove her wrong so he could feel better about himself. I pointed my index finger at him and said, "Look here, Kennedy, Adrianna is my friend and a damn good woman. Don't be trying to use her to prove a point or stroke your damn ego." I began poking his chest. "If you hurt her in any way, I'll whoop your ass."

He pushed my hand away, rubbed his chest, and whined, "Stop poking me, it hurts."

Sounding like our father, I told him to shut up and man up. "I'm serious, Kennedy. I don't give a damn about you knowing martial arts. I'll still beat your ass."

Kennedy held up his hand in surrender and said, "Okay. If she accepts my number, I'll take her out on a few dates. If things don't work out and she still feels the same way, we'll go our separate ways. I promise." He opened his car door and hopped inside. "Just give her my number, okay?"

"Okay, but I can't promise you she'll use it."

He started his car and said, "If she declines, then invite me and her to the next gathering so I can talk to her."

"All right, drive safe."

We gave each other dabs before he drove out of the parking lot and into the darkness.

I pulled my cell phone out my pocket and dialed Adrian's number.

"What's up, Omar?"

"Hey. Kennedy wanted to know if he could he have your number—or I can give you his. He wants to talk to you and try to make up for his rude behavior tonight if it's okay with you?"

Adrian blew air into the phone and said, "Omar, didn't I tell you I don't want to have anything to do with him?"

"I know you did, but he wants to talk to you. He wants to show you he's not the type of person you think he is. What do say? Yea or nay?"

"I really don't think this is going to work out, Omar, and I don't want to waste any of my time trying to make it work."

"I understand that." I decided to press her once more. "He said he wanted to take you out on a few dates. Will you give him at least one date please?"

Adrian sighed heavily "All right. I'll do it for you, Omar."

I smiled and said, "Don't worry. If he hurts you, I'll beat his ass for you."

She laughed. "Thanks in advance. Good night."

"Sweet dreams."

Read Between The Lines

It took a week for Adrian to finally utilize Kennedy's number and another week to go out with him. I was happy she had at least decided to give it a shot.

It was going on the fourth week after their first date, and I had to know how things were going. I'd been working in another part of the factory, I hadn't been able to chat with her much. So I invited her to lunch so I could get the info.

Adrian waved and smiled at me as she walked into the Applebee's a few blocks from the factory. She gave me a dap as she sat in the chair facing me. "What's up?"

I smiled at her and said, "What's up with you? How's things going with my brother?"

She took off her work hat, grabbed the hair band from her wrist with her teeth, and answered, "It's going good, I guess?"

I watched her fumble with her hair until she got her ponytail in the right position. "Didn't I tell you to stop wearing that hairstyle? Why won't you just keep it down?"

"I can where my hair any way I please, whether you like it or not. And I don't like wearing it down; it gets in my face when I'm working. Besides, I'm comfortable right now." She paused. "I'm thinking about cutting it short."

I gasped. "Noo don't do that! Keep the ponytail if you have to, but don't cut it." I loved her long, sleek hair. Sometimes I just want to run my hand through it just to feel the silkiness in my hands.

She giggled. "It'll be more of a trim. Shoulder-length, maybe."

"I guess I can deal with that." The waitress brought our drinks, I ordered a burger while Adrian ordered chicken tenders. I waited until she had walked away to ask, "So is Kennedy treating you right, or do I need to make a stop by his house when I get off?"

Adrian laughed. "There's nothing to worry about at the moment. He invited me to his house for dinner this week."

I teased, "Dinner at the house, hmm?"

She cut her eyes at me. "What's that supposed to mean?"

"Nothing. Just sounds like things are getting more

serious than I thought they would."

She smirked and said, "This isn't a 'Netflix and chill' thing. I have no intention of having sex with your brother anytime soon. Besides, I haven't even kissed him yet."

I frowned in confusion. "It's going on a month—why haven't you kissed him?"

"I'm taking things slow. There's no need to rush things, especially when I don't know how far this thing's going to go."

I wondered why she was still doubted the relationship when it was just starting and what it would take to get that feeling out of her head. "Listen, I'm not saying my brother is perfect—no one is—but he really is a caring and loving guy. Just roll with it. You never know, you might love him."

"Why are you determined to make this happen between your brother and me, Omar?"

"I'm doing this because I want to see you with someone who makes you happy and gives you joy and keeps a smile on your face. You've been single for like two years—you don't want to be alone for the rest of your life, do you?"

"What if your brother isn't able to do all those things? What if he isn't the one for me? I do have other men in my life that make me feel that way."

"Oh yeah? Who are they, other than your father, brothers, uncles, and grandfather?"

She looked at me, smiled, and said, "I got you."

The waiter brought our food.

I couldn't help but blush and smile back at her. "I'm proud to be a part of the team, but unfortunately I can't give you everything you deserve because of my situation. But that doesn't mean Kennedy won't be the man to give all of that to you. Listen, I can't make you feel or do anything you don't want to do. But you can't keep pushing guys away . . . you never know how things will turn out."

Adrian gave a heavy sigh and said "I'm not hungry anymore" She waved the waiter back over to table and asked for a to-go box. She put her hat back on her head, stood up, and said, "You're right, it is an unfortunate situation and I can't do nothing about it. I have to get back to work. I guess I'll see you around.

Confused about her action I frowned and asked, "Where are you going? And what do you mean, you guess?

Adrian paid for her food. "I'll be on the night shift until I finish my finals exam."

Trying to understand her emotion I said "Oh, okay. Well, call me when you can."

"Bye Omar."

Without another word, I sat in my chair and watched her walked out the door.

For some strange reason, it felt as if she were walking away from me. I didn't understand the discouraged tone in her voice or the dry goodbye. It had me feeling some type of way, wondering if I should ask Adrian what was wrong or if I should leave it alone. I decided to leave it alone because I felt as though I wasn't the cause of whatever was bothering her. I hoped she would be okay and tell me about it later.

***

"How's the food?"

Adrian wiped the tomato sauce from her lip with her napkin and said, "This spaghetti is pretty impressive; I can tell you used natural ingredients. The garlic bread was very good too."

Kennedy smiled. "My special ingredient's roasted tomatoes. Do you still think I'm jerk now?"

"I can't believe Omar told you I said that. And to answer your question, I'll say you are earning some brownie points for this dinner. Omar didn't tell me you could cook this well."

"You can't live your life off microwaveable and fast food—or have a healthy body with processed food."

"Omar told me you're a vegan and only eat organic."

"My brother seems to talk about me a little too much. What else has he told you about me?"

Adrian smiled. "He talks about you a lot because you're his brother and he loves you—the good, bad, and ugly sides of you." She paused. "He told me you had a rough life growing up, and that it has a lot to with the person you are today."

Kennedy frowned. "You believe everything my brother says to you?"

Offended by his question she said "Yes, I do. He hasn't lied to me, not once, since I've known him."

"Well, why don't get the answers straight from the horse's mouth so you can be 100 percent sure about that."

Adrian cleared her throat and said, "Okay . . . so did you have a rough time growing up?"

"I can't say it was rough—I grew up in a home with both of my parents, who were happily married for over twenty years. something a lot of my classmates and friends didn't have."

Adrian teased him, "The ones who used to beat you up and make you do their work for them were your friends? Or are you talking about the ones who made you do everything they said, no matter what it was, so you could be a part of their group—until your father came to school one day and whooped you in front of the class after he found out you cut class?"

Kennedy gasped, "I can't believe he told you that. I do *not* appreciate him telling my business without my knowledge."

Adrian noticed the anger in his voice and said, "Chill out, it's nothing to get upset about. It's funny to me. Trust me, you're not the first person that's happened to— and for sure not the last. Besides, it's those kinds of moments that make you grow stronger. Omar told me you do martial arts now and look at you, you are a successful accountant so be proud of yourself."

Kennedy finished the rest of his wine and gloated "You're right. I am bigger, better, and stronger." He grabbed the half empty bottle off the table, refilled his glass and added "Look who's laughing now."

Adrian arched her eyebrows at his cockiness and said, "You need to also remember a quote I learned in school, by someone name Winston Churchill said: 'You will never reach your destination if you stop and throw stones at every dog that barks.' Meaning don't waste your time trying to prove everyone that doubt you wrong—it will slow you down. Block the negativity and continue your journey."

What Changed?

EVER SINCE ADRIAN HAD MOVED to the night shift and started dating Kennedy, our communication and regular outings together had somewhat diminished. Lately, every time I tried to talk to her or hang with her, she'd been too busy.

The only reason I was able to see her on this particular night was because Kennedy's workplace was having a banquet and he'd invited Crystal and me to come.

I straightened my penguin suit while Crystal looked over her little white spaghetti-strap dress; with sliver diamond bracelets, necklaces, and earring, with her sliver and white Steve Madden shoes that matched. As the usher led us into the Event Hall

"Baby, does this dress make me look fat?"

I looked her up and down and said something I'd heard from a name Meech song: "You looking thicker than a Snicker, girl."

She frowned. "Are you calling me fat?"

"No, baby, I'm saying you look good. Stop overreacting."

She pressed her dress down with her hands and said, "I feel fat." She pinched her side and said, "Look at this fat."

I wanted to tell her she was doing too much. But that would only add on to the long line of arguments we'd been having lately—and the one she was about to start.

I shook my head in disbelief. I had no clue why females that weighed one twenty or less always thought they were fat. "Crystal, you pulling on your skin. There's nothing wrong with you."

She tugged on her dress. "I shouldn't have worn this. I'm not taking any pictures or eating anything but fruit and salad."

I rolled my eyes. "Crystal, if you really feel this way, why did you buy the damn dress?"

"It fit differently when I tried it on at the mall, Omar." She handed me her clutch purse and said, "Hold this. I need to go to the restroom to look in a mirror."

I grabbed her purse and replied, "Hurry up please; Kennedy and Adrian are waiting for us."

Crystal swooshed me away and said, "They can wait—and don't move without me."

I exhaled loudly, then glanced around the well decorated room with black and white décor, searching for

Kennedy and Adrian—well, mostly for Adrian. I spotted them near one of the food tables, chitchatting and laughing with each other. Kennedy had on his Brooks Brother's three button essential suit with a white vest and a black in white strip tie. While Adrian had on a long white evening gown with a slit up the side her leg. She had accessorized with black and white jewelry and shoes. I hadn't seen her new haircut until now. She had cut it to her shoulders like she said she would, usually wear it straight when it was down. This time, it was a little wavy. She looked like she could be on the cover of *Glamour* Magazine.

I wanted to rush over to her and tell her how good she looked, but Crystal was slowing me down. Adrian noticed me, tapped Kennedy on the shoulders, and pointed in my direction. I watched them hold each other's hands as they walked toward me.

Kennedy gave me a hug and said, "Thanks for coming, bro."

I smiled at him. "No, problem." Then I looked at Adrian. "You look amazing."

Before Adrian had a chance to say thank you, Kennedy placed his arms around her waist, pulled her close, and said, "The prettiest woman in the room." He kissed her on the cheek and she giggled, "Thank you." Kennedy let go of her waist.

Adrian straightened my tie. "You don't look so bad yourself, homey."

Crystal came out the restroom, placed her arm around mine, and said, "Hello. You two look great."

Adrian smiled politely and said, "So do you."

Kennedy placed his hand on Adrian's back and said "Come on, let me show you two where we're sitting."

We followed them through the crowd until we reached our table. The women sat, and I offered to get Crystal some food or a drink.

Kennedy announced that there is a salad bar. Appetizers, and an open bar. On the other side of the room.

Crystal looked at me and said "I'd like a spinach salad. Remember what I said: fruit and salad. I don't want no tomato, no onions, no olives. Light mozzarella cheese and Greek dressing but not too much."

I narrowed my eyes at her and said, "So you just want eat the leaves?"

I wasn't trying to be funny, but when Adrian laughed in response, I couldn't help but laugh with her.

Crystal stood up and grumbled, "I'll just do it myself, Omar."

I stopped her. "Sit down; I got it."

She shook her head no "I know you going to give me too much dressing. I'll do it myself."

I stepped to the side and said, "Okay, go ahead."

She pressed her clutch purse against my chest. "Hold my purse until I get back."

"Could you bring me something too?"

Crystal huffed, "Get it yourself."

With Crystal's purse in my hand, I sat down in my chair.

Kennedy asked Adrian if she'd like anything else while he went and got something to drink. She shook her head no and I jumped in, "Would you bring me some of those wings and a glass of Patron on the rocks please?"

Kennedy nodded and glanced down at his watch. "The award ceremony will begin soon; I'll be right back."

As soon as he walked into the crowed, I looked at Adrian, smiled, and said, "Soo, who is this glamorous woman sitting beside me? How come I never seen you look this good before?"

"I do this occasionally. Plus, this is an award ceremony—I had to look good for my man."

I acted surprised. "Oh, so he's your man now? You're claiming him now?"

She smiled and said, "Yes, I guess your little plan worked out."

"I guess it did. Everything seems to be going well."

Adrian sipped her water before saying, "It really is. Better than I expected."

Before I could ask another question about her relationship, she started talking about work. "Did you hear the rumors that some employees will be getting the pink slip? The union might be striking soon because of the pay cut."

I frowned. "No who told you that?"

"One of the drivers. Aren't you a part of the union?"

I nodded. "But I haven't heard anything about a strike. Maybe it *is* just a rumor."

Adrian sighed. "If it's true, I might as well pack my bag and go back home to Puerto Rico, because you know Mr. Pumer's care about me ."

I furrowed my eyebrows. "Are you serious about leaving? What about school?" *What about me?* is what I really wanted to say.

"I forgot to tell you—I passed all my tests! I'm just waiting to walk now. I might go home until then."

"Why didn't you tell me? We could have gone somewhere to celebrate."

"I'm sorry—I've been tied up with Kennedy. We can do it some other time."

"How about we go to a show or something?"

Adrian smiled. "That sounds good, but first I have to see if Kennedy has anything planned so we can double-date."

When I'd said "we," I was referring to me and her not Kennedy and Crystal too. "I was talking about you and me, Adrian. Like it use to be, we haven't hung out in two months, you don't call me anymore, and you always busy." I didn't know why her response had hit my emotions so hard. I didn't mean to get upset, but it was pissing me off.

She looked at me with a questioning expression. "Why are you getting upset, Omar? I can't do the things I used to do with you as much anymore. When I was single, it was cool—but I'm with Kennedy now, and my time is going to be spent more with him than you."

I growled, "I liked you better when you were single."

She giggled. "You wanted me to be happy, right?"

I mumbled, "Yeah." I wanted her to be happy, but not to point where she'd push me out of her life.

Adrian tried to comfort me my grabbing my arm and saying, "No matter what happens, I'll always have your back, Omar. We still cool, right?"

I gave her a half smile and said, "Yeah."

Kennedy was taking too long *with* my drink.

***

"I see you decided to lower your standards and give her a chance."

Kennedy looked over his shoulder at Crystal and replied, "I Gave Adrian a chance, yes. Lowered my standards, no."

"A couple of months ago, you said you wouldn't date a woman like her—that you wanted a woman like me."

Kennedy glanced at Adrian and Omar, then turned his attention back to Crystal. He laughed. "I never said that I wanted someone like you. My relationship with Adrianna is going very well, if you must know."

Crystal picked a strawberry from her plate bite out

of it seductively, and said, "Remember what you said? Don't settle or get too comfortable—there's always something better out there for you."

***

For me, the rest of the night w dull. I was on my second drink and patiently waiting for Kennedy to receive his awards so I could get the hell out of there. Seeing my brother holding hands with Adrian was making me sick.

Crystal seemed to be in a touch mood, too, for some reason; she was holding on to my arm like a leech. I swear it was going numb. Frowned at her and said, "Crystal, ease up on my arm, all right. I'm not going anywhere."

She pouted. "Excuse me for wanting to show my man some affection."

I glared at her and said, "Stop that." It might have been the alcohol talking, but I leaned over and whispered, into her ear. "When we get home, you can touch all over me as much as you want; just chill out for now, okay?"

She smiled and said, "Okay."

That kept her quiet for the rest of the night.

Kennedy finally got his award for his outstanding achievement with the company, after only being the or six years.

The ceremony was almost over.

Adrian decided to discuss plans for everyone to get together. She looked at me and said, "There's a Bad Boy concert coming the week after next—we should all go."

Crystal frowned. "I don't do concerts. Too many people, and all you can hear is the overly loud speaker bursting noise into the air."

Kennedy agreed, "I don't do too many of those either."

I looked at Adrian and said, "I'll go with you. I'd love to see Mase and the group 112."

She smiled at me and replied, "I guess it's just me and you, homey."

Kennedy looked at her and asked, "What day is it on?"

Adrian told him and he said, "I bought tickets to that show you wanted to go to; it's on that day. I was going to surprise you with them. The tickets are nonrefundable."

"Oh, wow! Thank you, Kennedy, I totally forgot about that." She looked back in my direction and said with joy "Omar, STOMP is back at the Fox Theatre. I know you enjoyed it when we went the first time. You should come with us."

Crystal frowned. "When was this? I don't remember you going to the Fox Theatre, Omar."

I looked at her and said "You was out of town with one of your friends."

She said "Oh, I'd love to see it this time."

Kennedy shook his head. no "You can't the show is sold out."

Adrian pouted at me and said, "Sorry, Omar, maybe next time."

The DJ began to play some slow melody music, and a few guests walked to the dance floor. Kennedy asked Adrian to dance, and she replied yes. I watched his hand slide from the to the lower part of Adrian's back and wondered if his next move would be on her peach-shaped butt. I slipped my drink and waited. His next move wasn't her butt, it was her hair I cursed to myself as he ran his fingers through it, then whispered something into her ear that made her giggle and playfully hit him in the chest.

I knew I could do the same to Crystal, but she wouldn't dare let me touch her hair the way he just did; she'd make sure I had her beautician on speed dial the next morning.

I knew I was supposed to be happy for Adrian and my brother; I was the reason they were together. But deep down inside, I wished things hadn't work out between them. I wasn't jealous—I just felt like he was taking her away from me, taking my time and place in her life.

Trying not to let my emotions get the best of me, I asked Crystal if she wanted to dance.

Getting frustrated as well, she declined "I'm ready to go."

I stood up and said, "All right, let's go."

The Switch-Up

The DJ switched the music to a more upbeat song. I stopped in my tracks when I heard him say, "At the count of three, I want everybody in the place to be, to make some noise if ya down with me! One, two, three": "Let Me Clear My Throat" by DJ Kool featuring Doug E. Fresh and Biz Markie began to play.

I looked over at Adrian, who seemed to be asking Kennedy for permission to do something. When he nodded his head, yes, she ran over to our table, grabbed me by the hand, and said, "Crystal, do you mind if I take him from you for a minute?"

She crossed her arms across her chest. and said "Yes, I do. We about to go."

"Hold on, baby, just one dance—this is our song."

Crystal sat down and asked Kennedy, "How do you deal with that on the regular?"

He looked at her and said, "They're just friends."

Crystal picked up Omar's half-empty glass of Patron and gulped it down. "Too friendly, if you ask me."

Kennedy stayed silent as he watched Omar and Adrian laugh with and hug each other. As they ran to the dance floor hand and hand.

Adrian took off her heels and said, "Come on, Omar, here comes my favorite part."

I chuckled and followed her to the dance floor. We danced and sang along: "Ya'll know us, we know ya'll represent yourself if you having a ball!"

We laughed together as I pointed at her and she

49

pointed to herself as the DJ yelled, "Puerto Rico people! Black people! White people! All people."

When the song was, over I bent down on one knee helped Adrian put her heels back on.

She wrapped her arms around mines We walked arm in arm toward them, and Crystal grumbled, "It's about time."

Ignoring her, I smiled at Kennedy. "All right, bro, you can have her back. Crystal and I got to go."

I hugged him and Adrian and then said to her, "Remember what I said: Don't disappear on me. We'll get together soon."

She gave me a dap and said, "Okay."

I walked over to Crystal, grabbed her hand, and said, then said my goodbye.

Adrian waved goodbye, then looked at Kennedy and asked, "You want to dance some more?"

He handed her... her purse and growled, "Don't you think you've done enough of that for tonight?"

Adrian frowned. "Are you upset with me because I danced with your brother? I asked you if it was okay and you said yes. It's not like we was bumping and grinding on each other, Kennedy. What is up with the attitude? I've told you before: there is nothing going on between Omar and me." She grabbed his hand and said, "The party's not over yet. Come on, let's dance."

Kennedy exhaled heavily and rubbed her knuckles with his thumb. "I'd rather go home if you don't mind."

The Switch-Up

Adrian hugged him, kissed him on the cheek, and said, "Okay, let's go."

***

"The party ended well, don't you think?" I asked as I locked my front door, then flopped down on the couch.

Crystal stood at the door with her arms crossed. "Yeah, for you."

Trying to ignore her attitude, I slouched down on the couch, placed my hands behind my head, and flapped my legs like wings. "What's your problem now? Are you upset because I danced with Adrian? I asked you to dance first, and you told me no, Crystal."

Not wanting to argue, I tapped my thighs and teased, "You want to dance, come over here and dance. You supposed to be touching me all over my body, remember?"

She growled at me. As she walked passed, I reached for her, but she pushed my hand away. "Don't touch me."

"Come on, Crystal. You know you blowing this shit all out of proportion. You act as if you just saw us kissing or having sex or something. We were just *dancing*. There's nothing going between us."

She placed her purse on the kitchen counter and said, "You think I didn't notice the way you looked at her the whole night? Like you were heartbroken over Kennedy's relationship with her? You looked like you wished you were in his place. What's up with that, Omar?

I didn't realize my emotions had been that obvious. I sighed. "It was nothing. Their relationship was just a surprise to me, that's all."

Crystal frowned. "How's that, when you were the one who hooked them up?"

"To be honest, Adrian didn't like Kennedy. She said he was arrogant and that she wanted nothing to do with him."

Crystal's ears perked up like an animal listening for its prey. "Are you saying she don't want to be with him? How are they still together?"

I arched my eyebrows. "I guess he changed her mind. She says she happy, and that's all that matters right now."

Crystal smirked. "I can see in your eyes that you're lying. Why is that, Omar?"

I rolled my eyes. This was the reason I didn't bring Crystal around any of my female friends. As many male friends as she's been around, I've never accused them of being more than that. I could mention the flirting I saw her doing with Kennedy at the food table. But I guess I could understand her assumption about Adrian and me; my actions were speaking louder than my words. "I know what you thinking, and I assure you there is *nothing* going on between me and Adrianna."

Smirking she said, "Prove it."

I frowned at her. "What you mean, prove it? If you're asking me to stop talking to her, that's not going to happen. I don't think it would be fair for you to ask me to do that when I told you we're just friends. If you feel you can't trust me, then you're free to leave."

Crystal walked over to me, sat on my lap, wrapped her arms around my neck, and said, "You're right. I'm sorry. Will you forgive me?"

I shook my head. "You gotta stop the nagging and bickering you've been doing lately."

She kissed me deeply and said, "Okay, let me make it up to you." I let her pull me off the couch. "Come on, let go to the bedroom I owe you a dance and a whole lot of touching."

Did Not See It Coming

Another month passed before Adrian and I finally got some alone time together.

I waved at her as she walked into Longhorns restaurant in a sundress and heels. I stood, gave her a hug, and said, "Looking good."

She smiled as she slid into the booth. "Thank you."

I sat back down and said, "I was waiting for you to order." I handed her a menu and waited a few moments while she perused it. "What you want to eat?"

She placed her purse down on the table and replied, "I'll just eat a salad. Kennedy's taking me out for dinner later."

When the waiter came to the table, I ordered a steak for me as well as her salad and then turned back to Adrian. "I see things are still going good with my brother?"

She looked at me and said, "How come every time we get together, all you do is ask me about my relationship with Kennedy? You know I like to keep my relationships private, no matter who it's with."

"I ask because I want to know if I need to kick his ass or not," I joked.

"No, Omar. Leave it alone. Why do you treat him like a red-headed stepchild? I told him some of the things you've said to me about him. He seemed pretty bothered by it."

I smiled. "He's just being a big baby, as always. It's no big deal."

Adrian sighed. "I think it is a big deal to him, and I think you need to be more considerate of his feelings, especially because of what he's had to deal with in the past."

I swoosh a hand, dismissing her concern, and said, "He'll be all right. Let's talk about something else. What do you think today's meeting going to be about?"

The waiter returned with our food.

Adrian dug in to her salad and said between bites, "Rumor has it there are a lot of undercover things going on. It might be about the stuff I told you about at Kennedy's award banquet."

At that moment, my phone rang. I pulled it out of my pocket, looked at it, turned the ringer's volume down, and placed it face down on the table.

"Why didn't you answer?"

I continued to eat my food and said "It's just Crystal." I continued eating my food. "She's been calling me all day since she knows I'm with you."

Adrian frowned. "She doesn't trust you with me?"

Not wanting to go into details, I said, "It's nothing to worry about."

"Then why won't you answer your phone, Omar?"

"I don't want the drama right now. I told her I had to go to this meeting today."

Adrian finished her salad and said, "You making the situation worse than what it is. Call her back, Omar."

I growled as I picked up the phone from the table and pressed the callback button.

"Why you not answering my calls, Omar?"

"I was eating. What's the problem, Crystal?"

"I was calling to remind you about dinner tonight. We are still going, right?"

I looked at my half-eaten steak and said, "Umm, yeah. Where do you want to go?"

"I want to try this vegan restaurant on Peachtree Street."

I frowned. "Since when did you become a vegan?"

"You know I'm trying to lose weight, Omar. One of my friends told me to become a Vegan."

I rolled my eyes and shook my head in disbelief. I'd told her a thousand times there was nothing wrong with her—that she should just exercise on the regular and eat healthier. I even agreed to do it with her, and she told me no because I'd push her too hard.

I exhaled loudly and said, "All right, Crystal, I'll pick you up after I go to this meeting."

"I'll meet you there because I need to go to the mall for a few things. How long will your meeting last?"

"Maybe an hour or an hour and a half. I'm not sure."

"I'll call you when I'm done shopping. You should be done by then."

"Okay, Crystal, bye." I pressed the end button and noticed Adrian glaring at me. "Why are you staring at me like that?"

"What's wrong with you, Omar? Why are you being all grouchy today?"

It was Crystal. She was really starting to get on my nerves with this diet thing and wanting to know my whereabouts when I wasn't with her. Everything Crystal said after Kennedy's award ceremony was a bald-faced lie, and since that night, she had gotten ten times worse.

In fact, that night had been the last time we'd had sex. We'd never gone a month without sex. I couldn't get a quickie, no hand job, no head—all because she said that was all we did and that we needed to spend more time with each other outside the sheets rather than between them. I didn't know where the hell she got it from or who she'd been talking to. Trying to be a good man, I decided to support her during this little journey and see where it led.

I finished eating my food, then said, "It's nothing. I

don't want to burden you with my problems. I'll be all right."

Adrian raised her eyebrows. "Burden me? When did your problems with Crystal become a burden on me?" She paused, and then asked, "Does it have anything to do with me?"

Not wanting to tell her the truth, I shook my head. "I just don't want to talk about it."

Adrian frowned "It is about me, isn't it?"

I really didn't want to talk to Adrian about the situation because I knew it would make her feel some type of way, like she was starting to now. I continued to give her the half-truth. "I don't really know what's going on. For some reason, she's decided she wants to change things."

"Like what Omar?"

I sighed. "Just becoming vegan and spending more time together and things like that."

Adrian added, "And spending less time with me?" I looked at her and she continued, "I know what I'm saying is true because I got the same lecture from Kennedy."

Surprised, I said, "Really? What did you say to him?"

"He told me he didn't feel comfortable with our friendship and I him told that if he feels as if he can't trust me, he can leave and I'll move on."

I frowned at her and said, "I don't want you two breaking up because of me—especially since you say you're happy now."

Adrian beamed at me and said "I can't be happy

without you in my life in any way, shape, or form, Omar."

I blush at the brightness of her smile, gave her a dap, and said, "Thanks, homey, that means a lot to me."

I glanced at my watch. "Time for the meeting."

***

Adrian had been right about everything when it came to the meeting. Corporate was talking about cutting people loose and people's hours because they went over their budget for the year."

"Now I know this will put some of you in a bind. We'll do our best to keep as many of you as we possibly can," Mr. Pumer explained.

"Who's going to get fired?" one of the drivers questioned. "It better not be me—I been here too damn long."

Some of the other employees agreed and began talking to one another.

Mr. Pumer held up his hands to get our attention and said, "Hold on. I know we have some good workers and some of you have served over ten years in this factory, but this is out of my control. I know how you guys feel because my job on the line too."

"I heard ya'll started paying these rookies more than us vets got when we first started, and that's how ya'll ran out of money," another employee who was also a vet for eight years. Announced, causing an angry roar from the room.

"That's not true." Mr. Pumer said nervously "Everyone we hired was brought on because of skill and experience. . .. We just over-hired a little, that's all."

Jamale, an overnight driver, asked, "When ya'll going to start cutting people so I'll know what I need to do? I got a family to feed and bills to pay."

Mr. Pumer looked at him and replied, "We're trying to straighten everything out so you won't have to worry about that. In a few more months, corporate will make their decision. We'll have another meeting in two month. Until then, everyone just stay calm."

I looked at Adrian with fear and said, "I can't believe this is happening."

Patrick, another employee who was part of the union, tapped me on the shoulder and said, "We going to have a meeting with the CEO ourselves. If they don't fix this mess, we're going on strike!"

I gave him a dap and agreed with him even though I wasn't with it. I wasn't mentally prepared for a strike or getting laid off.

"Don't worry, Omar," Adrian said, as though she'd been reading my mind. "You not going to lose your job. You're a great worker, and you've been with the com pany too long for them to fire you."

I walked with her to the parking lot and said, "I hope you're right, because I don't know what I'll do if I lose this job. I really don't want to start over." When we reached my car, I leaned against the hood.

Adrian placed her hands on my shoulders. "Don't worry, you won't have to."

I looked at her for a minute before saying, "You taking this lightly because you got backup. I don't."

She grabbed my face with both hands and said, "Listen to me, you have gained so much experience from this job. You'll find another job, maybe even a better one. You can start looking now so you're ahead of the game. And don't forget—you do have a degree in business management. That's *your* backup."

I looked into her dark brown eyes and saw how much hope she had in me and how sincere she was. Since I couldn't kiss her like I wanted, I pulled her close and hugged her tightly.

She rubbed my back and said, "I got your back. Everything's going to be okay."

I kissed the of her head and said "You just do know much you means to me."

We hugged for about another minute before she let me go and said "I hate to leave this like but I have to get ready for my date with Kennedy."

She was park next to me so I walked her to the driver side. Open the door for her, she steps in and said "Stop worrying, everything going to be ok. Call me later if you need too."

"Okay. Enjoy your dinner" I closed her door then watch her drive away.

Ain't Nothing Changed

I WAS TEN MINUTES LATE TO MEET CRYSTAL at *Herban Fix* vegan restaurant. I slid into the booth opposite her while she nagged me about being late: "Why are you late?"

"I was in traffic."

She picked up a menu and said, "I've already ordered me the organic kale simmered in curry laksa, and lemongrass consommé with vegetable dumplings."

I made what I liked to call the "doodoo face" at her: my nose and upper lip joined as one and rippled up like the skin of an English bulldog puppy.

She glared at me and said, "Stop looking at me like that. I'm going to order you the nape cabbage, mushrooms, carrots, fungus, and quinoa roll."

I scowled. "I'm not eating no damn fungus, Crystal."

She frowned. "It's a mushroom Omar."

"I'm not eating that."

"Come on, Omar, just try it. You might like it. Try

something new."

"Have you ever eaten that crap before?"

"No, but it'll be fun to try it."

The place cost fifty dollars a person, if she throws any food away I swear I was going to snap. "Don't order me anything, Crystal. I'm not eating it."

She pouted as she placed the menu back on the table. "Fine, Omar. All I wanted was to try something new and fun with you."

I exhaled loudly. "Crystal, don't start arguing with me. I'm not in the mood."

Growling she said "What is your problem? Why you so angry? And What happened at that meeting?"

The waiter brought her food to the table, and her frustrated expression turned into a smile. "Mmm—looks so good."

I smirked and declined when the waiter asked me if I would like to order anything.

Crystal grabbed her spoon and said, "Come on, baby, just taste it."

I shook my head no and watched as she scooped up a little of the kale from the curry laksa, nibbled on it, and said, "It don't taste that bad."

While she sipped on her soup, I continued our conversation: "I might not have a job in a few months."

She stop sipping her soup, stared at me and said, "What do you mean, you might not have a job? How did you lose your job? What did you do?"

I frowned. "I didn't do anything and I didn't lose my—the company is doing a budget cut, and they have to let some people go. The union's talking about going on strike until the issues settled."

Crystal poked at the lemongrass consommé, finally took a bite of a dumpling, and then immediately spit it back out into a napkin. "OMG! God, that is so disgusting." She gump down her water and said, "I'll order something else." She waved the waiter to the table and asked for curried rice with noodles, mushrooms, and seasonal veggies.

The waiter returned with that plate and I watched her pick at it. I grabbed the menu and couldn't believe she'd just made a forty-dollar tab with only damn soup. They had buffet but she didn't use it.

"Why would they fire you?" Crystal turn her nose up when she added "I can see your little friend getting fired since she hasn't been there that long."

I ignored her face expression when she talked about Adrian and said, "Everyone's job is on the line, especially if we go on strike."

"I told you to find another job a long time ago." Crystal wiped her mouth with her napkin. Without sympathy, she said ask "Now what are you going to do?"

She was on the verge of pushing the right button to set me off. She was really working on my nerves with her smart-ass comments. "I don't know what I'm going to do. I'll start looking for something else until this is settled."

Crystal continued to eat her food. "Well, let's just hope everything works out because finding another job won't happen overnight."

The waiter came to the table with the bill. I reached for it, but Crystal grabbed it and said, "I got it, because Lord knows you need to save every penny you got right now."

I growled at her, "Crystal, do *not* play with me. Give me the damn bill."

She grabbed her credit card out of her purse and said, "I got it, Omar. Trust me, you'll thank me later."

I snatched a hundred out of my wallet for the bill and tip and tossed it on the table. "I'm out of here." Sliding out of the booth, I said, "I'm out of here, don't follow me, call me or come to my house tonight."

She scoffed "Fine! Bye!"

***

Kennedy watched Adrian stare off into space as they sat in *Rathbun's* restaurant. "Adrianna, I told you not to worry about your job. You're about to graduate soon, so you'll be okay."

She blinked a few times, looked at him, and said, "I'm not worried about me, I'm worried about Omar. He's really nervous about losing this job."

Kennedy sipped his wine and said, "He'll be all right too. He has gained a lot of experience with that company; I'm sure he won't have a problem finding another job in that field. It would be better if he had some experience in his college major. This is why I say don't settle, always have a plan B, and be prepared for anything. It's a good thing you have a backup plan so you don't have to deal with the aftermath if the company goes bankrupt."

Adrian smirked. "Actually, I have to deal with aftermath too. Even though I'll have my degree soon, I don't have a job in my field yet. Omar and I are in the same boat."

Kennedy let out a heavy sigh and said, "You should've got a job as a dental assistant instead of working in that factory. It was such a waste of time for you and Omar."

She looked at him and asked, "Why are you so judgmental toward your brother? When Omar speaks of you it's with proudness and joy. But when you speak of him it's with envy."

Kennedy scoffed, "Everyone always taking up for poor Omar, but they call me the weak one."

"What's that supposed to mean?"

He looked Adrian in the eyes and said, "You'll never understand."

If I Was Your Man

Two weeks had passed since the announcement at work, the employees were quitting and getting laid off from left and right. The meeting with the union hadn't gone well, so they will be striking soon. I felt like I was stuck in the middle I didn't know if I was going to quit or fight with Union. I tried to get in as many hours and overtime as I could.

I was stressing out big-time. I still had the money our parents had left us and money in the bank, so it wasn't like I was in a sinkhole—it was more like a pothole. I could still survive for a little longer without Kennedy trying rescue me. Even though he called me and told me he would help me out if needed. I'd been searching for a new job and was just waiting on replies.

I hadn't talked to Crystal since our dinner after the meeting. She'd been calling and leaving messages, but I wasn't trying to hear them. All I wanted to do was sit back in my La-Z-Boy recliner and drink my Patron.

Which was what I was doing at that moment, on my day off. Hopefully I wouldn't be like Ice Cube in *Friday* and get fired on my day off.

I had just poured my second glass of Patron when my doorbell rang. I grimaced as I stood to answer it, praying it wasn't Crystal.

I looked through the peephole, then opened the door with a smile. "What's up, homey?"

Adrian ran her hand through her hair and mumbled, "Hey, may I come in?"

Concerned, I stepped aside to let her in. I knew something was wrong—she never came to my house without asking first because she knew Crystal might be there. I closed the door behind her, and she stood in the middle of the living room, looking lost. She looked around the room.

"Don't worry, Crystal's not here. What's up? You look stressed." Her face was red and eyes were puffy.

Adrian let out a large breath of air and said, "I just got cut."

I frowned, not understanding. "What you mean, 'cut'? Are you okay? Did someone attack you or something?"

She shook her head. "No. I got laid off."

I gasped, "Oh no! When did this happen?"

Adrian sat down on the sofa and replied, "About an hour ago, when I went in for my shift."

I sat beside her, hugged her, and said, "I'm sorry this happened to you."

"I'll be all right. They're giving me six months' unemployment. Two others employees received the pink slip, too. Mr. Pumer said I could finish my shift, but I chose not to. Why waste anymore of my time."

I sighed and agreed with her. "Right, does this mean you're going to stay here? Six months doesn't seem that bad. Besides, by then you'd have graduated and found a job."

"I don't know what I'm going to do anymore, I should've been doing something in my field, like Kennedy was constantly telling me to do."

"Did you tell Kennedy already?"

"Yes, I told him before I came here."

"What did he say?"

Her eyes watered up as she said, "We broke up."

I couldn't tell if she was about to cry because she just got fired or because Kennedy broke up with her. I assumed it was both.

"What was his reason? What did he say?"

"He said he can't pretend to be happy in the relationship anymore and that he can't see things getting any better between us. I tried to make it work—I really did." Adrian's emotion changed from hurt to anger. She stood up, then growled, "I should've just stuck with my gut and stayed single!"

I shook my head in disbelief and felt somewhat to blame for this. "Stop saying that, Adrian. You don't want be single—I know you don't. You are a good woman. You are smart, attractive, and dependable. Everything a man needs and wants."

She frowned and said, "You men don't know what the hell you want. You all always go after fake hair, fake booty, fake breasts—stuck-up, money-hungry bitches. When things go wrong or not as planned, you all say, 'Where the real women at?' You men are all the same."

I don't know why, but it sounded like she was talking about Crystal. I did agree with her that us men don't know what we wanted, but we weren't all the same. I know I might sound like a hypocrite because of my situation with Crystal. But I swear on my parents' graves that given the chance, I would never treat Adrian the way I treated Crystal because they were nothing alike.

"All men are not the same, we've known each other for years, and I've never steered you wrong. You have been nothing but good to me, and I treat you like you should be treated. If I was your man, I wouldn't treat you that way."

She looked at me as a tear fell from her cheek and said, "That's the problem. You're not my man." She ran her hand through her hair again, walked toward the door, and said, "I gotta go. I'll call you when I decide if I'm going back home or not."

Before I could stop her or say anything else, she was out the door, in her car, and driving out of the parking lot. I cursed to myself as I flopped down on the sofa and began punching at the air, fighting it as if I could beat down the temptation I felt to chase her and show her I could be the man she needed in her life.

I stood up and grunted in frustration. I grabbed my phone off the coffee table and dialed Kennedy's number—I had to find out what happened. I needed to hear both sides of the story. After getting voicemail, I tossed the phone on the sofa. I'd have to deal with him on another day.

If It Ain't About The Money

ANOTHER WEEK HAD PASSED, and the factory workers were still on pins and needles. I was trying hard to stay in the game, but the union was on its last straw; the strike would be starting any second, minute, or hour.

I placed my hands behind my head and stared at the ceiling as I lie in my bed. I exhaled heavily as I thought about Adrian. I hadn't seen her since her last visit I talked to her in few days, ago she had told me she was going back home this weekend but planned to return before graduation the following month. I'd told her to stop by before she left so I could say goodbye.

I hadn't gotten the full details on what happened between Adrian and Kennedy because my brother wouldn't answer or return my calls. He was probably avoiding me because he knew I was going to kick his ass.

I looked down at Crystal, whose head lay on my chest, and sighed again, causing her to wake up and look at me with groggy eyes. "Baby, what's wrong?"

"I can't sleep."

She rubbed my chest and seductively "You ready for round two?"

I stopped her and said, "I'm good." I wasn't in the mood to have any more sex with Crystal. The wham-bam-thank-you-ma'am sex I'd had with her just a couple of hours ago, hadn't solved any of my problems.

She scowled. "Are you still worrying about that job? I told you: just relocate, or don't strike with them and work."

I growled, "I told you I can't do that work while I'm on strike—I'm part of the union."

Crystal frowned. "You can still work if you want to. They can't stop you."

"Yes, they can—by fining me for breaking my contract. And I don't have the money or time for that."

I pushed her head off me slowly and sat upright.

Crystal turned on the lamp on the nightstand closest to her and said, "What about those job interviews you went on last week? What happened with that?"

I grabbed the remote off the nightstand and turned on the TV. "I didn't take them; they didn't pay enough for the experience I have."

Crystal stared at me and said, "You don't have time

to be choosing right now. You need to get what you can while you still have a chance."

I ignored her comment and flipped through the channels on the TV, trying to find any thing to block her out before I snap on her. Because she wasn't being understanding she was starting to piss me off.

"You should have got a job in your field like I told you—then you wouldn't be broke and dealing with this bull." And then she crossed the line. "You need to stop being lazy."

The words traveled from my brain to my mouth and flew out before I could stop them: "Shut the hell up, Crystal."

Shocked, she gasped, "I know you didn't just tell me to shut up." She hit me in the back of my head. "How dare you disrespect me!" She jumped out bed and said, "Don't you ever speak to me that way again!"

I watched as she began to put on her clothes as if she was about to leave—and as if I was about to stop her. I stayed frozen in my spot and remained silent. I know I was in the wrong for telling her to shut up, but I couldn't believe what she had said. I had disrespected her, but when this whole time, she'd been talking to me all reckless.

She grabbed her keys from the nightstand. "I'm going home."

I continued to stare at the TV screen still searching for something to watch. I said, "Get there safe."

She leaned across the bed and pushed me upside the head. "You are such an asshole, Omar. And don't expect me to come back over here anytime soon, either."

I barely asked her to come over anyway, unless it was for sex or going somewhere. Since she'd cut me off, there wasn't any reason for her to be in my house. All the talk about spending more time together was bullshit. Anytime I brought up the situation at work—someone new who had gotten fired or quit—she would suddenly get too busy to talk. or do anything. And that being a vegan shit went out the window with it. I'm assuming she was trying to copycat someone and it hadn't worked out the way she'd wanted it to.

Crystal crossed her arms across her chest as she stood on the side of the bed and yelled, "Omar! I can't believe you aren't going to stop me from walking out this door!"

I rolled my eyes, looked at her, and said, "Do whatever you want to do. I can't stop you from leaving—the choice is yours. I don't care what you do because I don't want to be bothered with you right now."

"What are you trying to say? You don't want to be with me anymore?"

To be honest, I didn't know what I wanted to do with her anymore. In the beginning, it had been her look, sex appeal, and spontaneous ways, but I was getting bored. I wanted more: someone who was more supportive, more compassionate—everything I wasn't

The Switch-Up

getting from her.

I didn't know how to tell her my feelings without causing even more conflict, so I tried to sugarcoat it. "Crystal, I'm going through a lot right now with my job, and my mind isn't clear. This constant bickering with you about everything isn't helping the situation. I think we should give each other some space."

"I do not constantly bicker with you!" She frowned. "And you don't do nothing for me anymore."

I frowned back at her. "That's a lie, Crystal. I do whatever you say, when you say it. What the hell have you done for me lately?" Before she could answer, I answered for her: "Not a goddamn thing! You see the stress I'm going through with work, and not one time have you came to me and said, 'Hey, baby, everything's going to be okay. I got your back.' If you cared for me like you say you do, you would be helping me up instead of putting me down. Damn!"

Crystal put down her things, crawled across the bed toward me, grabbed me by the face, gave me a peck on the lips, and said, "I'm sorry, let me make it up to you."

I knew this would lead to sex, and I didn't want it. Let me correct that I did want it, just not from her. I turned my head when she tried to kiss me again and said, "I'm tired of hearing that from you. Nothing changes; you just keep getting worse and worse."

She climbed on top and straddled me, wrapped her arms around my neck, and said "Come on, baby, don't be mad. I've been stressing out too. You know I've been working hard to get a job with the CDC. I know your job is taking a toll on you right now, but I can't let that stop me from fulfilling my dreams. Let me get myself together—then I can focus on you. If you go on strike, it could be months before it's over. Omar, what I am I supposed to do? Take care of you and your bills on top of my own since you won't accept a job offer with another company? Only God knows why you choose to stay with that factory."

"Crystal, I have enough money to take care of my own business until this is settled. I don't need you to take care of me; I just want you to work with me, not against me."

She scoffed, "I can't sit around waiting on you while you waste your time with this job when you could be working someplace else."

I couldn't believe she had turned my problem into hers—like mine didn't exist or matter as long as hers got solved. I moved her off of me, stepped out of the bed, and said, "Get out my house. I'm done with you! I've never known anyone as selfish as you. You act as if you been doing this shit by yourself! When I met you, you had nothing because your parents kicked you out and said you couldn't come back until you learned how to grow up and do shit on your own. I helped you get your house; I helped your money-hungry ass when you couldn't pay for school supplies because you maxed out your credit card on your hair, shoes, clothes, and other bullshit.

"Not once did I disrespect you the way you've been doing me lately. I might not have the suit-and-tie job you want me to have and you might make more money than me, but that doesn't mean I can't take of business!" I walked to the closet, pulled a suitcase out, and said, "I was doing just fine before you, and I'll be even better without you! Here is you a bag, now pack all your shit! It's over. I don't want to be with your ungrateful ass anymore." I stopped what I was doing and glared at her for a minute. "You disgust me."

Crystal's mouth dropped. She stared at me, speechless and in disbelief. I had never verbally talked to her that way—only in my head. I felt her pain when she began to cry uncontrollably, saying in broken words, "I, I, I dis, disgust you?" She sobbed so hard that her words sounded like squeals. "Is, is that how you really feel about me?"

I'd never before heard her cry so hysterically that she squealed. It was an unpleasant sound, and I didn't want to hear it again, so I told her I was sorry. "I didn't mean to say you disgust me."

"Do you hate me?"

"No, Crystal, I didn't say that."

"Do you wish you never met me?"

I sighed and rolled my eyes. There she goes always playing the victim. "I didn't say that either."

She wiped her face with the back of her hand and asked, "Do you really want to break up with me?"

"Us separating is the best suggestion I have for us right now." I picked up the suitcase, placed it on the bed, and said, "Goodbye, Crystal."

Guilty Pleasure

ANOTHER WEEK HAD PASSED, and I was officially on strike. I was surprised I was taking it so well. I really need break from the factory—I haven't taken a vacation in two years. I prayed the strike wouldn't last more than a month.

I sat in my car as I waited in the driveway for Adrian to come out of her house. I planned to take her to dinner and a movie since she was flying home in the morning. She stepped outside and locked her door, then smiled at me as she walked toward the car. She wore denim capris and a shirt that said "Live wild and free."

I hadn't asked her any more questions about her and Kennedy. And I still hadn't gotten a chance to ask him why he broke up with her like she was a bad habit. I didn't know if he was hurting from the breakup and just didn't want to be bothered, or if something else was going on.

I was surprised I hadn't heard from Crystal either.

Adrian stepped into my car and said, "What's up, homey?"

I leaned over and gave her a hug. "What's up? I missed you."

She put on her seatbelt and said, "Right back at you."

I started the car and glanced over at her. "How you been? What's new? How you feel?"

Adrian pulled the hair band off her wrist and said, "I've been doing just fine. I'll be feeling a lot better when I get home to my family."

I watched her put her hair in a bun; it had grown since she'd cut it. "No, no, don't start doing that again. Why do you keep doing that?"

She giggled. "I told you because I'm comfortable wearing it that way. Why are you overreacting?"

I drove out the driveway and replied, "Because I like it down. You have that Pocahontas thing going when it blows in the wind."

Adrian laughed loudly. "Thanks for the compliment. Where are we going?"

"Dinner and a movie."

Adrian looked at her watch. "How about just dinner? I can't be out too late—I have to get up early for my flight tomorrow."

"What time you want to end the night?"

"No later than ten thirty."

I glanced at her and said, "But it's eight now. I'll

only have two hours to spend with you before you leave me forever."

Adrian giggled. "Oh my god, Omar, you know you're exaggerating. I'll be back before I graduate."

"All right, let's just get takeout and go back to your place and make it a Netflix-and-takeout food night."

"We should do it at your house—I cut off my cable until I come back. If that's all right with you and Crystal."

I cleared my throat. "There is no more Crystal."

Adrian arched her eyebrows and said, "Really? What happened? When?"

"Last week. She couldn't handle that I wouldn't have a job for a while."

Adrian frowned. "But the strike just started." She raised an eyebrow. "I don't understand how you two lasted this long. You don't have any kids, nor do you plan on marrying her. So why were you with her for so long?"

I glanced at her for a moment before answering, "Have you ever heard this story before? A snake was hit by a car. A woman picked it up. Fed it and got it back to its full state of health. One day it bit her, injecting her with its deadly venom. On her deathbed, she asked the snake, 'After all I've done for you, why did you bite?' And the snake responded, 'You knew I was a snake when you picked me up.'"

Adrian smiled. "Yes, I have."

I drove the car into the Mr. Everything Café parking

lot and said, "Crystal was the snake; I was the woman. I knew from the first day I met her that she wouldn't be good for me, but I couldn't resist her look. In this case, venom was the sex."

We both stepped out of the car and after a moment, Adrian said, "I see."

I changed the subject back to work. "I heard Mr. Pumer got fired today, which means they'll have some better positions open when the strike is over. I'm going to apply for the one."

"That's a great way of thinking! I can see you getting whatever position you apply for."

I placed my arm around her shoulders as we walked toward the restaurant's entrance and said, "I appreciate you having faith in me. Thank you."

"You should take Mr. Pumer's job with his lazy ass."

I chuckled. "I might do that, seriously."

Adrian cheered, "That's the best news I've heard all day."

I laughed and then opened the door and said, "Let's get that food."

***

After eating and watching a movie, I looked over at Adrian sitting on the other end of the couch and said, "So this is what it like being single: sitting around watching Netflix all day."

She smiled. "It's not that bad. It means you're now free to do whatever you want, whenever you want, with whoever you want—without having to ask for permission first or deal with any consequences."

I had told myself I wouldn't bring my brother into our conversation, but I had to know how she felt about the situation. "Is it really over between you and Kennedy?"

Adrian sighed. "Yeah, it's done and over. There's nothing to work out—he made this decision, not me."

"I don't understand why. What happened? I thought you two were happy together."

"Apparently, he wasn't, Omar. It was just for show."

"Has he tried to call you or anything? Because I can't get in touch with him."

"No, I haven't seen him."

"I apologize for pressuring you to date Kennedy. I knew he was hard to deal with, but I thought if he had a woman in his life he'd calm down and it would maybe solve some of his problems."

Adrian exhaled "No need to apologize. It was my choice to go date him. I have no regrets." She paused and then continued, "But I can say; having a woman is not Kennedy's problem. It's something way deeper than that."

"I know he still has wounds to heal, but he's twenty-nine—he should have let all that shit go by now."

"Easier said than done, Omar, especially when

wounds can't heal because the person hasn't stopped picking on them. I think he needs to go back to counseling, and I think you should go with him."

I scowled. "I don't need any more counseling. I didn't need it the first time we went. Kennedy was the one losing his mind. Blaming me for everything wrong that happened in his life. After three years of counseling, I thought we was back to normal. I guess I can ask him what his problem is when I see him."

Adrian smiled. "I knew you would try to do the right thing." She glanced at her watch. "Oh, look at the time. I gotta go."

I frowned at her as she put on her shoes, not wanting her to leave. "Are your bags packed and ready to go?"

"Yeah, I just have to make sure I didn't forget anything."

"Stay here. I'll go get your things and take you the airport in my morning—what time's your flight?"

"It's at six. If you're going to my house, you might as well take me with you."

I complained, "Come on, Adrian. I don't want you to leave yet. You can sleep here—I have a guest room. We can leave by four so you can get your things, then I'll drop you off at the airport. We haven't spent any time with each other in weeks, and now you about to leave."

Adrian rolled her eyes and said, "I'm not dying, Omar; stop acting like a big baby."

I gave a little laugh. "So trying to spend more time

with my best friend before she leaves is being a big baby?"

She raised her eyebrows. "So, I'm your best friend now? No more 'homey'?"

I smiled and said, "You're more than a homey to me. You are a true friend. You tell me you have my back all the time, and you prove it to me every time we're together. I appreciate that with all my heart—and all that makes you my best friend."

Adrian blushed "Well, thank you for the upgrade. That was sweet." She leaned over and gave me a hug. "Okay, I'll spend the night with you, but you better not make me miss my flight."

I watched her stand up and said, "I won't, I promise." There was still one more thing I needed to know—an important question I couldn't get out of my mind. "Did you sleep with him?"

"Who are you talking about? Kennedy?"

I smirked. "No, the boogeyman—of course my brother."

She laughed. "No, Omar, I did not have sex with Kennedy. Are you happy now?" She grabbed her phone off the table and said, "I'm about to go to bed; I need something to sleep in."

I stood up, "I'll get you something clean. Toss your clothes in the washing machine when you get out of the shower. I'll put them in the dryer for you, too."

Adrian walked toward the bathroom and called back, "Okay, thanks."

I walked into my bedroom and grabbed a t-shirt and a fresh pair of boxers. I heard the shower water run, walked to the bathroom door, knocked, and said, "Here you go."

She cracked the door open and thanked me again.

I went back to living room and watched another movie. she returned to the living room twenty-five minutes later.

Adrian put her clothes in the washing machine, walked into the living room, and asked, "Omar, are you and Crystal just separated or actually broken up?"

I looked at her long legs and didn't see my boxers peeking out from the bottom of the t-shirt. "You didn't put the boxers on?"

She pulled up her shirt up to show the flannel boxers. "Of course, I did. I only sleep nude at home," she joked.

"Ha-ha, very funny. To answer your question, we broke up. Why you ask?"

"Because her things are still in the bathroom. Is she coming back?"

"She's supposed to come and get that stuff soon."

"You say y'all broke up last week. . .. Are you sure she's not leaving her things here just to have a reason to come back and get back with you?"

I shook my head. "She agreed that we're separate, so I doubt that's what she's doing."

Adrian crossed her arms and said, "'Separate' doesn't mean it's over, Omar. It means some time apart

The Switch-Up

until you both decide whether you want to continue the relationship."

"Trust me, it's over between us. I'm planning on packing that stuff up and taking it to her tomorrow."

"If you say so." She sighed. "I need to use your charger."

I grabbed it off the coffee table and handed it over. "I'm seriously done with Crystal."

"Okay, if you say so. I'm going to bed. Goodnight, and don't forget to set your alarm. Or to switch my clothes over to the dryer."

"I won't forget. Goodnight."

After an hour of watching another movie, I decided to call it a night. After a quick shower, I went into the laundry room to put Adrian's clothes in the dryer. I pulled her clothes out of the washing machine and arched my eyebrows when I noticed her laces panties and matching bra. Not trying to be a pervert but unable to help myself, I ran my fingers across the fabric and imagined how it looked on her. I put it in the dryer, then lifted the bra up to examine it, then looked at the size tag. I mumbled to myself, "34C sounds about right." I ran my hand across the cups before tossing it in the dryer and pressing start.

I had to get some self-control. I walked in the bathroom I splashed water on my face and then looked at myself in the mirror, trying to figure out how I was going to get through the night knowing she was in my house alone, in my bed, on the other side of that door. The urge to climb into bed with her was killing me, reaching all the way down to my Joe boxers. I looked at the door when I heard her snoring and gave a little laugh. The girl had no shame in expressing herself. If I told her she snored like a congested walrus, she'd probably laugh it off and be like, "Boy, shut up, it's a natural thing and I can't help it." She never took what I said to her personally; that's why I liked her so much.

I looked back to the mirror and my smile vanished. The feeling I was beginning to have for her was so wrong but felt so right—well, on my end it felt right. I wasn't sure about her thoughts on the matter, and I couldn't help but wonder: If I climbed in that bed, would she let me hold her in my arms until the sun came up? If I kissed her, would she kiss me back? I didn't even want to have sex with her, even though I knew her body would feel satisfied afterward. I guess you can call it a guilty pleasure.

I didn't know if Kennedy wanted to get back with her or not. It had never been my intention to come between their relationship, but it had all happened so fast and unexpectedly that I honestly hadn't seen it coming. I don't know if we'll be together, go our separate ways, pretend it never happened. Will I regret possibly ruining a good friendship by trying to cross the line and enter romantic territory?

I meant what I said when I told Adrian she was more than just a homey; I wanted to be with her.

The Switch-Up

I took a shower, then went into my room and closed the door. I tried to stop thinking about her sexually, but my mind wouldn't let me. I close my eyes as I lie in bed and imagine that she came in my room in the middle of the night and climbed on top of me, kiss me. I imagine me taking things further by taking off her t-shirt and letting down her hair so I could run my fingers through it. I imagine gripping a handful of it in my hand and gently pulling her head back as I plant hickeys on her neck, causing her to moan and grind on me. I massage her nipples between my fingers and suck on them until she started to grinded harder and moaned my name: "Ooh, Omar, I love it! Don't stop!"

With every stroke, she gave I grew larger between her thighs I usually do a lot more foreplay, but it's been too long and I couldn't wait to get inside her. I imagine grabbing her hips and moan "Ohh, Adrianna, let me inside, I got to get inside."

I lay her on her back and kissed her deeply as I pull off the boxers as well as mines. I continue to kiss and massage her body until I was inside. Oh, my god she was tight and she felt so good.

I moaned as I slowly ease myself in and out of her walls. "Oh, Adrianna, I need you. Ahh, you feel so good!" I had to go deeper and faster— I need this badly, and I need it from her. I proceeded to do so until I saw her 34C breasts were bouncing up and down and hear her moaning, "Oh, yes." Her moisture felt like I was going into a bottomless sea. The deeper I went the more I lost my breathe, I gripped the sheets for support. Sweat began to form on my body, and my eyes begin to roll to the back of my head as I enter ecstasy.

She pulled me closer, and I can't stop moaning her name: "Adrianna! Ooh, yes, Adrianna!" Then I exploded.

The sound of my alarm brought me back to reality. I realized my hand was moist, sticky and inside my boxers. I curse to myself as I look at the semen on my hand, then hopped out bed, pulled my sheets off then tip toed to my door, hoping Adrian wouldn't hear me go to the laundry room. I cracked the door and waited to hear if she was awake. I heard her alarm goes off, then stop. I let out a sigh of relief, speed-walked to the washing machine, and toss the sheets in before ducking into the bathroom. I took another shower and wondered if she heard me jacking off and moaning her name.

A moment later, she knocked on the door and yelled "Let's go, slowpoke!"

I put on my robe and call back, "I'll be ready in a minute."

After taking her home to get her things, we hit the highway towards the airport. Traffic was light, so she had plenty of time to get through security and make her flight.

I glanced at her as she sipped on her Mccafe coffee that she got from McDonald's before we got on the highway. She looked like she had a full eight hours of sleep and I look like I just took a catnap. I smiled at her and said "I can see you wake up flawless like Beyoncé."

Adrian smirked "Whatever, I look a mess. Do you not see these bags under my eyes? I didn't get any sleep last night because of you."

Thinking that she heard me moaning, I said "I apologize. . .. I usually have more self-control."

She glances over, confused, and said "You need to have self-control to know when to turn down the volume on the TV when you have a guest sleeping in your house, Omar?"

I gave a little chuckle "Oh, no I thought you—" I stopped my sentence before I put my foot in my mouth. "I apologize for that. From the way you were snoring, sounded like it didn't bother you that much."

Adrian laughs. "Oh my god, was I that loud?"

I chuckled "Like a congested walrus."

She placed her coffee in the cup holder before covering her mouth and burst into laughter. She laughed so long and hard tears started to come out her eyes.

I laughed with her and said "Breathe, girl."

I drove up to the drop-off section at the airport's entrance while she continues to giggle. I smile and said "Are you done? Because we're here."

Adrian unbuckled her seatbelt. "Okay, let me get out this car."

I stepped out the car, grabbed her bags from the trunk, and met her on the sidewalk. I placed the bags down and said "I'm going to miss you."

She smiled then hugged me and said "Me too."

I held her close and kissed the top of her head as it lies against my chest. She smelled so good.

She looked up at me. "I'll call you when I get there and when I come back."

She released me, but I held on to her hand and said "What am I supposed to do while you gone?"

"I don't know—maybe you can work things out with Crystal," she teases.

I smirked at her. "Ha-ha, very funny."

She glances at the entrance and said "I have to go." She hugged me again and kissed me on the cheek. "I'll call you later."

I sighed "Okay. Enjoy your flight, and I'll see you when you get back."

I waved goodbye as she went into the building. As I was stepping back into the car, Adrian ran back outside, smiled and said "I know what you did last night."

My eyes widen and I laugh with embarrassment. "You got me."

She giggled "Sweet dream!" then ran back inside.

I couldn't believe she took that lightly. Maybe she wanted it too, but I didn't hear her moaning or anything like that. Maybe she was and I was too loud to hear her. A car horn honking distracted me from my thoughts. Besides, I couldn't do anything with Adrian until I find out what's going on with Kennedy.

All Fair in Love and War

AFTER TRYING TO REACH KENNEDY by phone for the last time today, I drove home to clean and box up the rest of Crystal's things before I go visit him.

I inhaled the strong fragrance of Adrian's perfume in the guest room. "Damn, that smells good." She must have slept with some lotion on because the pillows smell like it too. I sniff one of the pillows before pulling the case off and putting it in the washing machine with the sheets.

I call Crystal to make sure she comes to get the rest of her things today—not tomorrow, or any other day. I got straight to the point when she answered the phone: "Crystal, what time are you coming to get the rest of your things out of my house?"

She scoffed "Omar, I told you I was coming to get it all soon."

"I need for you to come and get it now."

"I can't come right now."

"Why? You not working today."

She blew are into the phone and said "I'm busy right now, Omar."

"Crystal, I will leave your things on your doorstep if you don't come and get them in the next two hours."

She smacked her lips and said "Okay, bye."

I grab the box preparing to place it by the door, when the doorbell ranged. I shift the box from one hand to the other before answering the door.

"Where the hell you been, bro?"

Kennedy looked at me and said "I heard about the strike. How you hanging?"

I stepped aside to let him in and notice he was looking a little rough—I've never seen him in jeans and a plan white t-shirt. "I'm good. Who told you, and why haven't you been answering my calls?"

"Crystal told me two weeks ago after we ran into each other at a bar." Kennedy flops down on the couch. "I've been busy."

I placed the box on the kitchen table, more focused on my brother "Whatever," I walk to the couch and said "What happened between you and Adrian? Why you break up with her?"

Kennedy wiped his droopy face with his hand, inhaled and exhaled deeply then said "It just didn't work out."

I could tell he had been drinking from his body language. "Kennedy, have you been drinking? What's wrong with you?"

He growled "I'm fine, just tired."

"Hey, man, are you stressing over Adrian?"

"I'm not stressing about her—what's done is done." Kennedy stood up. "I did what was best for us." He takes a deep breath "I didn't come here to talk about Adrianna. I came here to talk about Crystal."

I frown. "What about her?"

He looked at me and said "She's no good for you. She's been trying to get with someone else for the last four months."

I swoosh him off. "I don't even care about that. She can do whatever she wants now. We broke up a week ago."

Kennedy sighed. "I know that, too."

He took two steps back when I started walking towards him. "What are trying to say? How do you know if I haven't talked to you?"

"I told you a long time ago to dump her, Omar. She's been trying to get with me since I came back here. I wanted to tell you sooner, but I knew you wouldn't listen."

I couldn't believe what I was hearing. Crystal has been chasing my brother this whole damn time. But I tried to make me look bad for the feelings I have for Adrian. "Are you trying to tell me you want to be with Crystal?"

He took another step back and said "I didn't come here to fight you, Omar, but we are together now."

I gave a little laugh and ask, "You're together now?"

Kennedy stood tall, as if he was trying to be tough. "Yes, we are, and we've had sex."

I was now in his face when I poke him in the chest with every sentence. "I can deal with the fact that you and Crystal are now together. I can deal with the fact that you screwed her." He flinches, squinting his eyes with each received jab. "But what I don't understand is how this all came about when you were supposed to have been with Adrianna!"

Kennedy pushed my hand away. "Stop poking me!"

I pushed him and yell, "Shut up! Did you cheat on Adrian!"

Kennedy grabs the arm of the couch to keep from falling. After balancing, "No, I didn't."

I grab him by the shirt, then push his back against the wall. "Stop lying!"

Kennedy growled and pushed me off him. "Get off of me, Omar! I swear, if you don't stop pushing me, I'm going—"

I smushed the side of his face with my and said "Do what? Tell Mom? She's no longer here." I poked his chest again. "Come on, be a man for once in your life!"

Kennedy let out a roar of frustration, then tackled me like a wrestler. We tossed each other around, knocking some furniture over and causing pictures to fall from the wall. I took a few blows to the jaw from him, and he took a few blows to side and stomach before I had him kneeling in front of me.

I wiped the blood from my mouth with the back of my hand as I stood up and said "You need to get a refund on those karate classes cause your ass is weak!"

I must have hit a nerve because the next thing I remember was him upper cutting and lifting me over his head, then slamming my body to the floor. I groan from the pain and he punched me in the jaw. He held me down by my neck, and I swear he was trying to kill me. I grabbed his hand and tried to twist away from him. "Kennedy, get the hell off me!" I stared him in the eyes as he huffed and puffed at me like a raging bull. I swear, his pupils had turned red. We've fought numerous times, especially when we were kids, but I've never seen so much hate in his eyes. I tugged on his hand and yelled "Kennedy! What the hell is wrong with you? Let me go!"

He stared me down for another minute before loosening his grip. He stood up, exhaled loudly, held out his hand, and said "I'm sorry."

I pushed his hand away and wobbled myself off the floor. "Was you trying to kill me?"

Kennedy straighten out his stretched-out shirt. "I

said I was sorry, I didn't mean to hurt you. Are you okay?"

I rubbed my back as I leaned against the back of couch. "Hell no, I'm not okay. You damn near broke my damn back!"

He stepped towards me and said "I'll take you to the hospital if you need me to." "Don't touch me." I slide my way around to the front of the couch and groaned as I lie back on one of the cushions, hoping to soothed the pain.

Getting worried that he might have actually broken my back, Kennedy pleaded. "Omar, come on. Let me take you to the hospital."

I closed my eyes. "Shut up talking to me, Kennedy. I don't want your help and I don't need your help. Get out of my house."

Ignoring everything I just said, he walked over to me. "Omar, listen to me, I did *not* cheat on Adrianna with Crystal. The reason we broke up was because she didn't want me." He pauses. "She wanted you."

I open my eyes, looked at him, and said "What?"

"She wanted you, O. The whole time we were together, all she talked about was you. I've seen the way you looked at her, and I know you want her too. That's why I let her go." Kennedy start telling me about the conversations he had with Crystal at dinner and the banquet. Everything he was saying went in one ear and out the other. All I could think about was the pain in my back and the fact that I could have made my fantasy about Adrian a reality—with no consequences. I closed my eyes back and said "Get out of my house, K."

As always, Kennedy tried to solve his issues with money: "I'll pay someone to clean this mess up, and I will replace everything. Please. Please go see a doctor; I'll pay for any medical bills. Okay?"

I growled "Whatever, Kennedy. Just leave my house and don't come back and take Crystal's shit with you."

The Switch-Up

THREE WEEKS HAD PASSED, and I was still jobless and I was still trying to repair my back. I didn't bother asking Crystal why she did what she did. After getting every string of her hair out of my house, I tried my best not to stressed too much about the job or any of the things that happen with Crystal and Kennedy.

All I wanted to do was see Adrianna. She was graduating today, and I was so happy for her. I placed her gift in the backseat of my car; I was running late but I mad it there just in time to see her walk across the stage. I cheered for her and a group of people did too; I assume they were her family members and friends. I haven't met all of them, just her brother and father, when the stalking incident happen. They came to town to check on her and thanked me for being there to protect her.

I waited outside for her after the ceremony; she was hard to find in the diverse crowed. I tried to go near any interracial couple A Hispanic man and an African-American woman. After a few minutes, I decided to stay in one spot hopping she would see me.

I hear a male voice call my name; I turned in the direction and saw her father coming towards me with a smile like the Kool-Aid man's. I shook his hand as he said, "Omar! It's good to see you here!"

"Same here, sir, it's good to see you again."

He wrapped his arm around my shoulders and said "Adrianna is with her mother; I'll take you to her. We're going to a friend's house to celebrate—you're more than welcome to come."

I walked with him through the crowd. "Thank you, sir, I would love to come."

As soon as we reach Adrian, she wrapped her arms around my neck and said "I was wondering where you were."

I hugged her tightly. "You know I wouldn't have missed this for anything in this world." I kissed her on the cheek and said "I'm so proud of you."

She giggled, "Thank you." Then she notices the few bruises on my face and asks, "What happened?"

Not wanting to ruin her day, I told her we'll talk about it later.

After celebrating with good music and food. I took Adrian back to her house and we talked about what happened between me and Kennedy while she's been gone.

I sat on a bar stool as she puts away leftover food in the kitchen. She shook her head in disbelief. "Kennedy and Crystal are together now? When the hell did that happen?"

"I don't know."

"So he cheated on me with her? I can't believe this."

Her getting upset made me think that maybe she really did care for Kennedy. "He said it happened after you two broke up."

She smirked at me and said "Yeah right. Those two planned this shit."

I watched her walk from the kitchen to the living room. I really wasn't trying to ruin her day and I really want to find out if what Kennedy said was true—does she really want to be with me? I have to tell her how I feel before her mind starts singing that "I don't need a man," "I can do bad all by myself" crap.

I turned around on the stool in her direction and said "Don't worry about them. You should be with me anyway."

She stared at me before asking, "What did you just say?"

I stared back at her and answer, "I want to be with you. Kennedy and Crystal deserved each other. I deserve you, and you deserve someone who's going to love you, support you, and cater to you—not to prove anyone wrong . . . only because he wants to." I stood up, walked over to her, grabbed her hands, and said "That's someone is me. Adrianna, you are everything I need in a woman. We've known each other for, it's been two years now, and through this whole friendship, you've shown me nothing but loyalty and support. I'm sorry I couldn't do this sooner, but I really want to make you happy, if you'll let me."

Adrianna blushed and said "Wow, Omar, that was a mouthful. I really don't know what to say right now. I mean, I would love to give us a shot, but I don't want it be this way."

"What way? What are you talking about?"

She lets go of my hand, sat down on the sofa, and said "As a rebound, Omar. You just ended a relationship of two and a half years less than a month ago. And you fought your brother over her."

I sigh. "Well, I wouldn't call it a relationship—it was more of a companionship. I wasn't fighting Kennedy over Crystal. I was fighting him over you, Adrianna." I held out my hand, and placed hers in it and pulled her to her feet, and said "Listen, I know it's hard to believe, and I know it may take a while to trust me, but I would do anything and everything if I could be the only person you call on when you need someone. Put a smile on your face." I reach for her pony-tail and let down her hair, then ran my hand through it. and said "Run my figures through your hair." I grabbed face gently and She kissed me, then giggle said "This is crazy. You hook me up with your brother, and I end up with you while your brother ends up with your girlfriend."

I held her in my arm and smiled "I guess you can call it *The Switch Up*."

The Switch-Up: Four Months Later

EVERYTHING BETWEEN ADRIAN AND I was going great. Four months has passed, and we were living on cloud nine. She'd got a job as an orthodontist, and I got promoted in the factory, as the new executive administrative assistant. Everything was perfect, and since Kennedy and Crystal are no longer a part of our lives, I wasn't expecting anything to go wrong.

I sat back in my La-Z-Boy recliner and watch TV, waiting for Adrian to come back from the grocery store so she could make me some dinner.

When I hear the knock on the door, I got up. I open it there it was: the storm that decided to rain on our parade. I looked at Crystal as she cried a river on my front doorstep.

"Omar, I need your help."

I frown at her. "Why?"

"Have you seen Kennedy?"

I haven't seen him since the fight. I stared at her before answering, "No, I haven't, I thought he would be with you since you two supposed to be together."

Crystal sniffs and said "He's not answering my calls and he's not at his house."

Thinking that he went back to LA, I said "He's got to be somewhere. When was the last time you saw him?"

"About a month ago." Her chin trembles. "I really need to talk to him. It's very important."

For some reason, I felt the need to ask her what's wrong. "Crystal, why are you standing her at my front door crying?"

She began to sob harder and said "I'm pregnant, Omar."

I shook my head in disbelief. "You got to be freaking kidding me!"

Coming Soon:

The Switch-Up 2